COLD CUTS

By

Robert Payne Cabeen

Omnium Gatherum
Los Angeles

For Cecile

Bones in a basement, a snake in a tree,
a rock on the moon, a ghost in the sea,
a face in a crowd, a rip in a sheet,
rust on a statue, a dog in the street.
Everything is somewhere,
so where are you now?

So Sad Man

A pernicious sadness squirmed into the man's bones and wormed its way deep into his icy marrow. The only emotional shard that remained of his shattered psyche was sorrow.

The sad man strained against his bonds, more out of habit than any real hope of breaking free. He unclenched his teeth, and gasped for breath. Nylon cord, cinched tight to his cot, restrained him, but the weight of his deranged captor crouching on his chest was the primary cause of his worsening asphyxia.

The maniac squealed with each desperate heave of the sad man's chest. He leered down at his flailing victim, wagging his gnarled finger in the man's face. He ranted on and on about imaginary plots hatched in the fever of his delirium. The sad man turned his head to avoid the noxious shower of rancid spit spattering his face with each wild accusation.

As his crazed captor's tirade droned on, the sad man tried to find his happy place. He had quite a few, but his happiest place was the alley behind Dixon's donut shop where he had his first kiss with Emily Stone. It was the only place happy enough to transport him away from the horror he had endured for so long.

The sad man clinched his eyes shut and found himself in the alley with Emily. She was so mysterioso, kinda witchy, with the morbid allure of Lydia from *Beetlejuice*. He loved the way she smelled. The scent reminded him of clove gum, licorice candy, and the flowers at his Aunt Vivian's funeral.

Emily pulled a jelly donut from a white, paper bag. It was obscenely oversized, deep-fryer fresh, dusted with powdered sugar, and oozing scarlet raspberry jelly. This wasn't just any donut, it was a pure white dove in the hands of a bewitching, dark angel, a concentrated offering. Emily raised it with reverence, and took a bite. Confectioner's sugar rained down on her lacy black blouse. Without thinking, he brushed the powder off. Emily pressed his hand on her chest, and held it there. Her heart beat quick and strong. She leaned forward and pressed her lips to his. They were soft and warm, with a trace of powdered sugar and raspberries.

It was his first kiss, and he wanted it to last forever.

He ran the tip of his tongue across her raspberry lips—they parted— tongues touched.

The vile taste of rancid fish assaulted his taste buds. The foul vapor of fetid breath rose in his throat, jolting him back to his cruel reality.

The sad man's eyes sprang open.

A tongue flopped around in his maniacal captor's slimy mouth—a herring in a sloshing bucket of chum. The acrid stench seared his nostrils. He jerked his head hard. His cervical vertebrae protested with a series of bubble-wrap pops.

The fiend's pursed lips, resembled a prolapsed anus with rotting teeth. He made sickening smoochy sounds as he stroked his captive's matted hair.

The sad man laughed and cried, at the same time.

A sardonic grin spread across the madman's cadaverous face as he leaped from his captive's chest.

The sad man gasped a lung-full of stale, icy air.

His tormentor circled the perimeter of the frigid, tomb-sized, room like a caged beast. The human monster scanned his surroundings, spied a large medical kit, and pounced on it. It was the kind a field surgeon would use. He riffled through its contents, and muttered to himself as he organized an ominous assortment of surgical devices on the cold concrete floor.

Neat little piles of sterile packages fanned out in a semi-circle at the maniac's feet. Their unwholesome purpose was a mystery to the sad man, but one thing was certain—whatever it was, it was going to hurt. A foreboding orthopedic saw took center stage in the sinister display. Its sharp, serrated teeth clearly had an appetite for flesh—and so did the maniacal fiend.

The maniac's crazy eyes burned wild in their hollow sockets. He glared at the sad man, licked his hideous lips, and chortled with inhuman glee.

Cryptic Communication

Frank Sayer sat at one of the mismatched Formica tables in the lunchroom and stared out the only window as he jabbed at a vending machine salad with a plastic fork. He looked over the heads of the jabbering staff and gazed out the window at a seagull perched on a sign outside the entrance of a single story industrial complex in Santa Cruz, California. The sign on a dead grass covered berm read: Environmental Defense International. The gull scanned the parking lot. It dove on a greasy, paper bag and scavenged a single, ossified French fry.

The bird danced on the hot asphalt, in the narrow space between a late model Prius and an older BMW, that hadn't been washed since the first season of "The Walking Dead." The gull rooted around inside the bag for another fry, pulled out a ketchup packet, pecked at it a few times, and flew away.

Sayer poked at the baby greens in his salad. The ranch dressing turned pink.

Fucking beets. I'd just as soon eat dirt.

He pulled on his collar to loosen his tie, and swallowed an unappetizing bite. What he couldn't swallow was the EDI board's mandate he start dressing his age. Sayer's flesh crawled inside his generic, blue suit. The organization he started in faded 501's and hiking boots had become a bloated, non-profit corporation with more money than passion.

He scanned the library-quiet lunchroom. His employees hunched over their cell phones while they ate. Occasionally, a muffled chuckle or a muted gasp broke the unsettling hush. Sayer longed for the days when the room would have reverberated with impassioned discussions about the environment and political action.

Why do I still do this? All these years. All the ranting about climate change—and then it did. We changed too. These kids still care. They do their jobs, but they're numb. I'm numb too. Every year it's the deadliest hurricane on record, the worst fucking flood—the biggest wildfire. I'm gettin' too old for this shit.

Fast footfalls echoed in the hallway outside lunchroom.

Terra Perez bounded through the door, set her briefcase down, and said, "Okay, guys, it's almost time." She dragged a rickety table under a wall-mounted television and hoisted a chair on top. She climbed up the wobbly contraption, and switched the TV on.

Terra radiated the kind of enthusiasm that gave Sayer hope for the future of EDI. Sometimes, he had to dial her back a bit—but not too much. She made him feel more like a stern father than a boss, or at least what he imagined what it would feel like if he were somebody's father. She reminded him of a Mayan maiden disguised in a smart business skirt. She was sexy, but didn't seem to know it. Terra looked young for her age, and at the same time much older. Maybe it was the contrast between her black pixie cut hair and her determined, dusky, umber eyes.

The young woman fiddled with a loose cable on the old TV.

Two L.L. Bean poster boys, Brad and Chad, sat at a nearby table. Their pastel, plaid shirts were prep school approximations of what environmentalists might wear. They enjoyed their view of Terra's practical panties a little *too* much.

"Now, there's one for the upskirt museum," Brad said scrunching his face mock agonized lust. He raised his cell phone to film Terra's posterior for posterity, as she balanced on the rickety chair like an acrobat.

Chad nodded. "No shit. You getting this?" He mirrored Brad's expression.

Fucking idiot donor's spawn. The things we have to do for money.

"Oh yeah. This is gonna go viral."

"Terra, come down from there." Sayer said, sounding like a high school principal.

Terra scrambled down and sat next to Sayer.

Brad and Chad continued to ogle Terra.

Sayer whispered in Terra's ear and told her what the guys were up to.

Her eyes narrowed, and she stormed over to the pervy prepster's table.

She slapped the palm of her outstretched hand, "Give it to me."

Brad snickered to Chad, "That's what she said."

Terra folded her arms, "Hand it over, Brad. I mean it."

"What?"

"You know what."

Brad and Chad pretended to be confused.

Terra snatched the phone from the table, "The code—*now*."

"I'm not giving you the code to my fucking phone."

"Suit yourself." Terra put the cell on the floor and raised her foot to smash it.

"Okay, okay. Give it to me. I'll put in the code."

Sayer could see Terra didn't need any help, but added, "Don't make me come over there."

Brad tapped in the code and handed the phone back to Terra. She watched a few seconds of the clip, deleted it and said, "Guess that's the first time you circle-jerks saw underpants without skid marks."

Brad and Chad stared at their food and smirked.

Terra turned her back on them and fiddled with the phone.

Brad rubbernecked to see what she was doing, "Hey. I'm sorry, all right. Gimme back my phone."

Terra tossed Brad's phone on the table and sat back down next to Sayer.

Sayer said, "If you want to file a sexual harassment report, I have all the—"

"No, no...not necessary. I got this." Terra grinned, "I sent one of his dick pics to his mother."

On the TV, a vaguely familiar voice narrated a documentary, "Antarctica, an angry continent on an angry planet." Massive sheets of ice calved from a monolithic glacier, and crashed into the sea. An ice blizzard raged.

Terra hopped up and addressed the room, "They're on right after the ice."

Co-workers scowled at her for interrupting their funny animal videos and important texts.

Footage of a modern science station on a desolate ice sheet filled the screen. The narrator continued, "Earthwatch One, a remote science station at the bottom of the world. Dr. Ozioma Pratt and Dr. Benjamin Eaton endure extreme cold and terrifying isolation to study the effects of global warming on Antarctica's fragile flora and fauna." On screen, two young-ish guys, wearing white lab coats, thumbed through stacks of photographs, inside a high-tech lab.

Ozioma Pratt was a big, big, mixed race lad, with a wise-ass smile and snickering eyes. Ben Eaton was skinny and fidgety, with wild red hair and a pasty complexion.

"There they are," Terra said, in a high octave.

Sayer glanced up, gripping the edge of his table.

On screen, Eaton nervously sorted photographs.

"On a mission from Environmental Defense International," the narrator said, "these two environmental scientists have uncovered a rash of mysterious mutations and mutilations."

Eaton held up a photo of a glowing mushroom and said, "Here's an anomalous evolutionary aberration—bioluminescent fungi."

Pratt pulled out a photo from his stack. "Hey, if you find glowing mushrooms disturbing, check this out." He held up a photo: the eviscerated carcass of a giant sea lion. "There's no explanation for dozens of large mammal mutilations like this."

Eaton butted in, brandishing a photo of a yellow growth on a slimy rock. "Several of the 200 species of Antarctic lichen have actually achieved a primitive form of locomotion. This mutated colony migrated five centimeters in two hours."

"Yes doctor, your creeping crud definitely seems to be on

the move. But what about *this*?" Pratt pulled out a picture of bloody whale parts scattered on the ice. "I don't know whether something actually hunted this whale down, or just scavenged it on the ice. Either way, there's a new kinda critter down here in Antarctica."

"How's that for media exposure?" Terra said to Sayer.

He forced a smile and grunted.

A singsong voice crackled on a loudspeaker. "Paging Frank Sayer, come to the communication center. Paging Frank Sayer..."

Sayer tried to wave the voice away. "Okay, okay, all right already."

All day long, one bogus emergency after another.

He draped a napkin over his salad and headed for the door. Terra grabbed her valise and followed. As they neared the communication center, curious onlookers peeked inside the cramped room.

Well that's a first. What's going on here?

Sayer and Terra elbowed their way inside.

Marcus, the too-hip VSAT radio operator, motioned for the crowd to be quiet. He pushed back his porkpie hat, adjusted his headphones, and scribbled on a note pad.

"This better be good," Sayer said.

The room fell silent as Marcus spoke into the microphone with his jazz DJ voice, "Earthwatch One, do you read me? Earthwatch One. Come in Antarctica."

"Those divas haven't filed a report in six fucking months," Sayer said.

Marcus threw down his headphones. "Damn, had 'em, but they dropped out. They're gone."

"Did you get anything at all?" Sayer said.

"Yeah, but it doesn't make any sense." He ripped the note off the pad and read it aloud. "I hate myself. I hate myself." Marcus waved the note in the air. "That's all folks."

Sayer grabbed the note. "What the fuck is this supposed to mean?"

"Hell if I know, Mr. Sayer. He just kept saying he hated his damn self," Marcus said.

"Which one was it?"

"Dr. Eaton, I think. He was trippin.' Moanin' and shit."

"I've had it with those lab-monkeys."

Sayer stormed into the hallway, with Terra close behind. They snaked through a maze of institutional hallways, past workers in cubbyhole offices, with computers displaying a variety of diversions and perversions—and occasionally some actual work.

"Dr. Eaton and Dr. Pratt are gathering critical environmental data down there, Mr. Sayer" Terra said, as they continued walking.

Sayer laughed. "You've been reading too many of your own press releases."

Her sincerity and enthusiasm were usually welcome, but sometimes they were simply maddening. "We're lucky to have dedicated scientists like them on our team."

"Get involved with a real project, Terra. Earthwatch One is window dressing."

"The fund-raising committee really got behind Earthwatch One." Terra brushed her hair out of her eyes.

"Because you got those young Frankensteins on the Discovery Channel," Sayer said.

He could tell by the look in her eyes she was passionate about this.

"At least Dr. Eaton called."

"To let us know he hates himself? Come on."

"We have to be supportive of our own guys," Terra said.

"Remember Project Mastodon?"

Those sons of bitches didn't file a single report in over a year.

"They would have cloned that woolly mammoth if the Genomic Institute hadn't—"

"Yanked their ticket like I'm about to do." Sayer crossed his arms and scowled. "The only time the Genomic Institute heard from them was when your boyfriend sent a requisition for more of his damn chocolate cupcakes."

"Ozzy isn't my boyfriend. He's a friend-friend." Terra's cheeks turned pink and she stared at her shoes.

"So, has your "friend-friend" contacted *you* lately?"

"Well, no. I think he's mad at me."

"About what?"

Did you eat his pork chops?

"I sent him an article about that paleo diet, and I haven't heard from him since. He hasn't returned any of my texts or posted anything online, like forever." In spite of her professional façade, she couldn't hide the fact that she was worried.

"I don't give a damn about their online presence. I expect timely reports. What the hell are they doing down there?"

Terra riffled through her valise and pulled out a folder marked *Earthwatch One*. "What about Dr. Pratt's radiation readings? They were off the scale."

"That was interesting six months ago." Sayer shook his head.

Terra dropped the folder. Black and white PR photos of Pratt and Eaton fell to the floor.

Sayer picked up the photos and yelled at them. "I'm going the fuck down there and bring you slackers back—dead or alive."

"To Antarctica?" Terra said with excitement in her voice.

"Yeah, Antarctica, and I might just drag your supportive ass down there with me."

"Really?" Terra's eyes widened with anticipation.

"If you want to freeze your tits off, be my guest."

Terra clutched her valise to her chest. "You bet I do, Mr. Sayer."

"You can handle the media. You know, damage control."

Because if anyone's going to cause damage it's those asshats.

"They could actually be in trouble, you know."

"Perfect. That's what you tell the press."

If we play our cards right we can turn this into a PR coup.

"But—"

"If we wind up doing this, we'll set up a press conference

and you'll tell them we're sending a rescue party to Antarctica."

"Thanks for taking a chance on me. I won't let you down." Terra ran off beaming.

"See how you feel once you're down there," Sayer called out to her, "And tell Marcus if he gets through to those geeks, they better fucking dazzle me with science."

Sanguine Salad

Sayer scanned the lunch room, but nobody looked like they wanted to chat. Their eyes were still on their phones. He looked up at the TV. The Discovery Channel was still on. A goose and a lion cub cavorted in a wildlife santuary.

I wish my staff had as much rapport as these interspecies friendships.

He glanced at Brad and Chad at the next table as he probed his limp lettuce with the plastic fork.

Except for those idi-holes.

Brad whispered to Chad and Chad looked accusingly at Sayer.

"Hey panty peepers," Sayer glared at them and grabbed his belt-buckle. "Wanna see my tighty-whities?"

"I would have thought Mr. Sayer would have been going commando." Brad said.

Chad spewed acid green energy drink from his nose.

Sayer chomped down on a fork-full of arugula.

Fucking idiots.

An electrical jolt of pain shot directly into his brain. He shot out of his chair, spit out a glob of bloody mulch, and stuck out his tongue. The throbbing intensified as he pulled a splintered plastic fork prong from the bloody gash in his tongue.

"Oh thit." Bloody saliva dripped down Sayer's chin and pooled on the dull linoleum floor.

Brad pulled out his phone and started filming.

Chad looked over Brad's shoulder at the screen. "Bro, gross."

The lunch crowd looked up from their phones, then looked

at each other until a dark-haired woman in a lab coat stood up.

Sayer lisped, "A little help here, pleathe."

The woman approached, a look of concern on her face.

Sayer held out his tongue to show her his wound.

The look of concern on her face deepened. The sound of a screeching eagle broke the awkward silence. The woman froze, fished her phone out of her lab coat and held up a finger. "Got to take this."

If I'd been a pelican covered in crude, she'd have rushed to my aid. No such compassion for the guy who signs her paychecks.

Sayer ripped out the jagged spike and wrapped his tongue in a paper napkin. It turned red instantly. He shouted at the open door, "Thankth a lot."

Aloha Antarctica

Six Months Earlier

Ozzy Pratt stirred beneath a *Star Wars* blanket on a cot in the Pit, Earthwatch One's living quarters. Ozzy wasn't claustrophobic, but sometimes the confined space made him feel like a submariner sweating out a depth charge attack. The Pit was 400 square feet of space planning on acid. Half the room was OCD tidy; the other half was frat house messy. His oversized cot was designed by NASA, but his blanket was designed by Target—for eight-year-olds. It was never intended for use in Antarctica, but it let Ozzy imagine he was staying warm inside the carcass of a Tauntaun on Hoth, the ice planet.

Ozzy rolled over and a widescreen TV flashed on. Anime exploded on the screen. The covers flew off as Ozzy bolted upright. He tossed back the hood on his red, footed jammies, ransacked the covers, found the remote, and zapped the TV off. He glanced over at Ben Eaton's cot. It was empty, and made up so perfectly a drill sergeant wouldn't even bother flipping a dime on it.

Alone for once.

Drs. Ozzy Pratt and Ben Eaton called their living quarters the Pit because it had been carved out, twenty feet below the surface of the ice, by a British expedition nearly a century ago. During renovation of the ice-bound cubicle, workers found a variety of culinary artifacts, a rusty tea kettle, tarnished silver cutlery, pewter plates, and a chipped porcelain cup.

There were also dozens of empty tins that long ago contained sardines, pickled eggs, even peaches in heavy syrup.

But the most exciting find was an unopened Huntley and Palmers biscuit tin. It was in excellent condition and beautifully lithographed. The gold ink still glittered through the oxidized patina. The contractor had presented it to Ozzy, as a joke when construction of their high-tech living quarters was complete. The contractor put the tin in an old fire alarm box, with "In case of emergency, break glass" stenciled on the front.

Ozzy kept the biscuit tin in a place of honor, surrounded by his impressive collection of action figures. Dozens of the plastic homunculi crowded the floor-to-ceiling Metro shelving that covered one wall of the Pit.

Ozzy's collection was as eclectic as it was sizeable. Figures from Action Man to Star Wars and everything between had ventured south to the coldest place on Earth. Not a single one still had its original packaging—a must for any serious collector. Ozzy wasn't serious about much and that included his collection. One of his favorite pastimes, back in the world, was going into a comic book shop, paying hundreds of dollars for a rare action figure and ripping it out of its packaging. As the shop owner looked on in horror, Ozzy would toss him the mangled blister card and say, "What good are they if you can't play with them?"

Ben Eaton, didn't share Ozzy's enthusiasm for vintage action figures. In fact, Ben claimed they creeped him out. He often complained that all those little eyes watching him all the time made his skin crawl. The worst offenders were the McFarlane horror movie figures. The worst of the worst were Clive Barker's Cenobites—and Ozzy had the whole *Tortured Souls* series. Ben had never seen *Hellraiser* because someone who never saw a horror movie said it was obscene and satanic. As annoying as Ben's screeds about popular culture were, Ozzy loved it when Ben referred to his figures as, *evil little effigies of a doomed civilization.* Ozzy looked over at his collection. Sure enough, Ben had turned all the Cenobites around facing the wall—as he did every night when Ozzy was asleep.

Ozzy planted his feet on the cold concrete floor, and braced himself for his morning battle with gravity. If he weren't a man of science, he'd swear the pull of gravity was stronger in the morning. He was stout and healthy, but he really felt his extra weight in the morning. After his coffee, a shit and a shower, he was master of the universe.

Ozzy lumbered to the hot plate and switched it on. The kettle was half full of water, so he turned his attention to a box of assorted, instant gourmet coffee packets.

One left. Damn. French Vanilla. I hate that shit.

He grabbed his favorite coffee mug, a rare Rumph, stoneware, Chewbacca tankard from the 1970s and peered inside Wookie's head.

No mold. Nothin' green.

Ozzy ran his finger around the interior, and scrutinized the dark brown powder that wafted away as he rubbed his thumb and forefinger together.

I'll rinse it out next time.

Ding.

Shit, I got mail.

Ozzy grabbed his laptop and checked his email.

Damn, it's Momma Iya. Did I reply to her last email? Yeah, yeah, I did. It was about some old Massai shield they won at a Christie's auction.

The kettle whistled. Ozzy made his coffee, took a sip, and winced.

I'll make some real coffee in the lab. This is just a caffeine delivery system.

Ozzy sipped his coffee with a sneer and read his mother's email.

> I hope you are staying warm, my dear Ozioma. I worry for you in that cold place too much. How come you do not email me more? Your father says not to bother you, because you have important work to do, but I cannot help wondering how you are doing.

Your father and I are having an article published in *African Arts Magazine*. It is all about the Songe tribe's Kifwebe masks. We have many beautiful photographs.

Your father wrote this not too long biography of us. He could not use many words. He wants to know what you think. Here is it.

Shanumi Akioya, a member of the Yoruba tribe, from south western Nigeria, and Andrew Pratt, a member of the Celtic tribe, from southern Ireland, met at an international tribal art symposium in Lagos, Nigeria. She attended as a cultural anthropologist from the University of Benin, and he as an African art historian from UCLA. Together, they conducted field-work throughout the African continent, and co-authored *Orisha Thunder: A survey of Yoruba Art and Religion.*

Let me know what you think. It must be sent soon.

Ni ife,

Momma Iya

Ozzy sighed and hit reply.

Momma—

It's cold down here, for sure. It doesn't bother me much though. I have plenty of extra insulation—ha ha. It's hard to be heavy in skinny town. It's always warm in LA, but down here in this frozen wilderness the extra pounds really come in handy. Most people can only stay out on the ice for 15 or 20 minutes. I can work for an hour or more. I could stay out longer, but after my nose froze and fell off, I have to be more careful. (JUST KIDDING)

Sorry I haven't emailed you more, but Dad's right. We've been super busy. There's so much to do, and so little time to do it. I'll catch you up when I get home. I miss your banga soup and ofada rice.

The bio sounds okay. The Celtic tribe thing was kind of funny. I'm sure the academics will think it's hilarious. Tell Dad that periods are free, and it wouldn't kill him to use them more often.

Love you both,

Ozioma

Ding.
Ah, there's one from Terra.
Ozzy tossed back the remainder of his candy coffee and clicked Terra's email.

Hey Ozzy,

Thought of you last night. Been missing our Friday fright fests. Watched *Suspira* by myself. Big mistake LOL. One word—maggots. You know how I hate maggots.

I know I promised no more diet talk, but I think this one might work for you. Have you heard of the paleo diet? You just eat like a cave man. If a cave man didn't eat something, you don't eat it either. I attached a PDF. Don't be mad. I worry about you.

Hope you and Dr. Eaton are getting along. I know he's annoying, but he really knows his stuff.

Miss ya,

Terra

C'mon, Terra, the paleo diet is so three diets ago. Gotta think of a killer comeback. I got it. I'll tell her there's a new diet Dr. Oz recommends. The Suspira diet. Eat all you want, but you have to swallow some live maggots with every meal. I'll take a selfie with a hand full of rice. That'll get her. No time now, though. Later.

Ozzy lumbered to the pile of his arctic gear on the cold floor and dressed with the determination of an astronaut preparing for a spacewalk. He patted his pockets and pulled out a Slim Jim. He pulled open the Pit's heavy steel door and stepped into the stairwell, cradling his laptop.

A single black feather hovered and twirled in a frigid vortex above Ozzy's head. He trudged up the icy stairs twenty feet to the ice above. When he emerged from the gaping cavity in the ice, a white whirlwind howled across the frozen desert. Ozzy could barely make out Earthwatch One's cluster of prefabricated buildings. The science station's domed structures, meteorological equipment, and storage sheds stood alone in the windswept wasteland.

What planet am I on, anyway? This looks like the ruins of

some lost civilization on a doomed planet. Come to think of it, maybe it is.

A dozen yards ahead, a blue light flashed above the door to the lab. As Ozzy headed for it, he stumbled into a slushy patch of snow and stopped. The swirling snow parted. At his feet, a dead seal lay gutted on the ice. This was a fresh kill. Condensation rose from the warm, wet blood pooling around the hollow carcass. Ozzy sidestepped the gore and headed for the blue light—much faster than before. In the distance, an eerie *screech* sliced through the polar wind with the clarity of an icy razor.

Ozzy shouldered the door open. The Slim Jim dangled from his lips as he headed for the lab.

Ozzy trudged down a narrow hallway. A trail of bloody footprints pooled on the insulated vinyl flooring. He stopped at the inner door to the lab, and peered in a small window. Inside, Ben Eaton huddled over a seal carcass on a stainless-steel examination table.

I swear, sometimes Ben looks just like Doctor Pretorius from Bride of Frankenstein, except much younger, with his frizzy hair and pinched features.

Ozzy bounded into a lab.

Eaton jumped, and dropped his scalpel. "Hell's bells, you could have given me a heart attack," he said, clutching the front of his white lab coat.

"You're jumpier than usual today."

"It's these mutilations. They're unnerving."

"Well, brace yourself. I found another one, and it was farm fresh."

"Where did you find it?"

"Right outside the outer door to the lab."

Ben put both hands on the sides of his head. "This is not good. This is not good at all."

"Ya think?"

"None of this makes sense. The only apex predator in Antarctica is the leopard seal."

"Seals don't eat each other," Ozzy said.

"Precisely."

"Any seal bites on the specimens?"

"Not a one. Take a look at this."

Ozzy wandered over to the examination table.

Ben removed a tissue sample from the seal's empty thoracic cavity with forceps and dropped it in a specimen jar.

Ozzy said, "Which one is it?"

"The Wendell you found last week."

The seal's ribcage was intact, but stripped of even the tiniest strip of flesh.

"Anything left inside this one?"

"Totally eviscerated like all the rest." Ben pried the rib cage open.

"Clean as a whistle," Ozzy said.

"Too clean."

Ozzy leaned closer for a better look.

Though the carcass exhibited no signs of decomposition, it smelled noxious, like rotten shrimp soaked in ammonia.

"Weird smell."

"Indeed, all the others smelled like that as well. I'm not certain what would produce such a pungent odor. Take a look at the numerous slashes in the bone. Quite odd, don't you think?"

"I don't get it."

"Take a look at this." Ben probed an empty eye socket with forceps and pulled out a stringy strand of tissue. "Notice anything funny?"

"Nothin' funny here, Ben." Ozzy leaned over Ben's shoulder.

"Not humorously funny. I mean peculiar. The optic nerve. It appears to have been severed—with surgical precision."

"What kinda animal could do that?"

"None I can think of. I'm not at all certain an animal did this, Ozzy."

"It's weird enough out there on the ice without mysterious shit."

"You should spend more time with me in the lab. I could use some help with the—"

Ozzy wiped the idea away with a frantic swipe of his

hands as he retreated from the examination table. "I'll take my chances on the ice." He took a deep breath. As he exhaled a lungful of lab air, he longed for the fresh scent of a salty Malibu breeze, or the wild flower potpourri of a canyon hike in the foothills north of Caltech. But his favorite scent of all was the way a dirt trail smelled after a rain. Even the streets smelled great after a good soaking.

Terra said there was a name it. Some fancy French word. Petri something. I'll Google it later. I'll bet the air in here is toxic as hell. It reeks of antiseptic, with a hint of eau de Ikea showroom from all those chemical laminates, adhesives, and pressed wood.

Ozzy wandered over to the coffee maker, and poured himself a cup.

Ben said, "Do you intend to double check those anomalous radiation readings from yesterday?"

"For sure. Must have been something wonky with the equipment." Ozzy blew the steam rising from his cup, took a sip, and spit it out. "What the fuck?"

That's not coffee.

Ben laughed and said, "Sorry, that's herbal tea, a hearty blend of goldenseal, horehound, and yarrow."

"More like a hearty blend of ass and ball sweat."

"I wouldn't know what ass and ball sweat tastes like, but you certainly seem to know a lot about it."

"Who would even think of putting that shit in a coffee maker?"

"I thought it was an excellent idea."

Ozzy pointed to the drip coffee maker, "What does that say?"

Ben sighed and said, "Mr. Coffee," as though he knew where this was going.

"That's right, Mr. Coffee, not Mr. Crazy Clown Tea."

"It's a proven fact that coffee is deleterious to your health."

"Bull shit. What's a proven fact is that coffee is a fucking magic elixir of health. Haven't you been reading all those studies that list all the horrible shit coffee prevents?"

"Coffee industry propaganda."

Ozzy opened his laptop and Googled, coffee studies.

Ben said, "Don't bother. Believe what you want. I know what I know."

"You don't know jack about coffee. So, what school did you go to?"

"You know, very well, I received my PhD from Harvard."

Ozzy scrolled down the search. "Okay, this study is from Harvard. Drinking coffee, regularly, reduces the risk of heart attack and stroke. Lowers the risk of developing type 2 diabetes. Then there's a laundry list of cancers. It even prevents—"

Ben clicked away the browser window. "I know what I know."

A selfie of Ozzy and Terra, mugging cheek to jowl, filled the computer screen. Ben looked confused.

"Terra changed her profile picture," Ozzy said.

"One of your adventures in Photoshop, no doubt," Ben said.

"No way. She likes me."

Ben frowned. "I can't imagine why."

"She thinks I'm cute—and funny."

"Ms. Perez is an intelligent, attractive young woman. She would never—"

"Kiss me goodbye at the airport?"

Ben pretended not to hear and headed back to the examination table. He organized his dissection instruments on a white, porcelain enamel tray, with his back turned to Ozzy.

"Don't walk away from me. We're not done here," Ozzy said.

"I'm too busy to listen to any more of this nonsense."

"Well, hear this. The next time you put that shit in the coffee maker, I'm gonna piss in the pot—not that you'd notice."

Silence.

"What do you think of that, Ben?"

"It's an excellent idea, Ozzy. Urea contains a surprisingly rich concentration of nutrients, enzymes, hormones, vitamins, antibodies, and essential minerals. Didn't they teach you that at Caltech?"

"I'm outta here." Ozzy closed his laptop, grabbed the keys

to the Sno-Cat, and headed for the inner lab door. He paused for a moment to see if Ben was going to say goodbye. He didn't.

Fuck him and his health-nut tea. He wouldn't last two minutes out there at fifty degrees below zero. The wires inside his mass spectrometer have more fucking insulation than he does.

Ozzy trudged down the hallway—flicking his Slim Jim like a cigar. An unfamiliar sense of dread intensified with every footstep. When he reached the outer door, he stopped and pressed his ear against its faux wood fiberglass shell. Ozzy half convinced himself the screech he heard earlier was just the wind. The cruel polar wind can be deadly, but it doesn't rip the guts out of seals.

Ozzy took a deep breath.

Aw, fuck it.

He zipped his parka and yanked the door open. Wind and snow rushed in as he hustled out into the cold, cold unknown.

Rads & Ruins

Out on the ice, miles from Earthwatch One, Ozzy turned his broad back toward the savage wind. He clutched a walkie-talkie as he adjusted the dials on a squawking Geiger counter.

Ozzy shouted into the walkie-talkie, "Hey Ben, I double checked those gonzo radiation readings from yesterday." Ozzy glanced down at his Geiger counter. "They're totally Chernobyl again today. Over."

Ben's voice crackled back, "What's the source of the radioactivity? Over."

Ozzy raised his field glasses. They fogged up whenever they got anywhere near his hot face, but he was able to see an ominous, black cylindrical object. It seemed to hover in the seamless expanse of white. There was no way to judge its exact size or distance, but one thing was certain—it looked like trouble.

"There's something sketchy out there. I'm going in for a better look," Ozzy said, his Geiger counter squawking louder as he plodded closer. "It looks like one of those portable nuclear reactors—cold war vintage—over."

"Get out of there."

"This baby's hot, over."

"You're going to get dosed."

"Roger that."

Ozzy retreated, still checking his Geiger counter. He plodded toward his ride, a beater Sno-Cat. Patches of snow speckled the mammoth, orange snow tractor. He stowed his gear, climbed in the cab and cranked the engine. It coughed and snorted, then sputtered to life. The steel beast lurched forward with amazing torque.

As the Sno-Cat rumbled across the ice sheet, Ozzy leaned toward a dash-mounted microphone. "Come in Veggie-wiener, this is Big Mac callin'. I'm a headin' home. Come on."

"Stop talking like a hillbilly," Ben said, "Just bring some provisions from the storeroom. I'm calling it a day. See you down in the Pit."

"That's a big ten-four, good buddy."

Ozzy reached under his seat and pulled out a crumpled bag. One petrified honey-roasted peanut remained. He gulped it down.

Inside the Sno-Cat, Ozzy searched under the seat for more tasty tidbits. He retrieved a filthy chocolate cupcake tray and licked the two brown circles.

After twenty minutes treading ice, he was almost home. The foggy windshield framed Earthwatch One. It wasn't much to look at, but it looked pretty good to him in the middle of the desolate Antarctic desert. Especially since it was the only thing visible in the bleak, white wasteland. Ozzy could almost taste the cream filled chocolate cupcakes waiting for him back at the lab. There were a dozen cases left in the storeroom. As far as he was concerned, when they ran out the mission was over.

Ozzy wiped the condensation from the windshield with his gloved hand. A sleek, snow vehicle screamed toward him. A plume of crushed ice shot out the back. It skidded sideways and stopped just short of a head-on collision.

Two men in white uniforms with red wolf patches jumped out.

Ozzy waved.

They didn't. Instead, they raised automatic weapons and fired full auto. Bullets ripped through the windshield of the Sno-Cat. Safety glass rained down on Ozzy. He dove to the floor.

The matched pair played a nine-millimeter duet on their Uzis, vivo fortissimo.

Ozzy didn't like the tune—too fast—too loud. He covered his ears and waited for the show to be over.

The lethal duo played everything they knew, packed up their instruments and headed for their vehicle.

Ozzy squeezed back in his seat, peered out the shattered rear window and watched the shooters speed away.

He grabbed the dangling microphone. "Shit. A cuppla parka boys just tried to blow me away. They—they had fucking machine guns."

"Who were they?"

"How the hell should I know? I didn't get their license number."

Ozzy sniffed the air and looked out his side window. Amber fuel pooled on the ice below the Sno-Cat.

Shit, shit, shit.

He struggled to open the bullet-riddled door. It was jammed. He tried the other—also jammed. Ozzy dove through the blown-out windshield frame. His belly wedged him in tight. He backed off, planted his feet on the seat, and pushed hard. He sailed across the hood, hit the ice, and slid like a huge hockey puck with no goal in sight.

Ozzy struggled to his feet and looked back. Flames rose from the underbelly of his Sno-Cat. A fireball erupted from the fuel tank. The steel beast spewed its mechanical guts. The scorched hood flew straight up and landed in a snowdrift like an orange tombstone.

Ozzy scanned the wreckage. Oily smoke billowed from every ruptured orifice, scribbling black graffiti across the pallid sky.

Another explosion rocked him from behind. It was bigger—much bigger. He whipped around. The shockwave sucker punched him in the gut. He gasped a breathless, "No!" The wind blew the word back in his face.

Debris from Earthwatch One rained down all around him. The force of the explosion snuffed out the flames at the moment of combustion. All that remained of the compound was smoking rubble.

Ozzy leaned into the glacial wall of wind and plodded toward his smoldering science station. Crystalline snow pricked his face like ground glass in a wind tunnel. The hysterical monkey in his chest rattled his ribs in hope of escape. He staggered through a maze of twisted metal and expensive junk, holding his side and gasping for breath. A mechanical insect, once an electron microscope, swayed in a web of tangled wires. Sweat sloshed in Ozzy's boots as he surveyed the smoking rubble in disbelief. Charred provisions and shattered equipment littered the ashen ice.

Ozzy called out for Ben as he trudged toward the Pit. He pointed a flashlight into the smoke-filled stairwell that led to their living quarters. He stumbled down the stairs that descended the twenty feet into the ancient ice. He stepped over a mangled storage drum, pushed the heavy steel door open, and staggered into the Pit.

Small patches of lichen glowed around the door. Ozzy's flashlight cut through the smoky darkness. Ben Eaton cowered, coughing in the corner. Ozzy maneuvered through an obstacle course of jumbled furniture to his dazed partner. He switched on an emergency light and threw back the hood of his parka.

Ozzy lifted Ben onto a chair. "You all right?"

"What's going on up there?"

"Everything's blown to shit."

"Was it those—those parka boys?"

Ozzy picked up pieces of a broken G.I. Joe from a pile of action figures on the floor. "Hadda be. After they finished with me, they headed south—as if they could go much further south."

"Any markings on their Sno-Cat?"

"Not a Sno-Cat, more like a snow Bugatti. Man, that thing was screamin.' Musta had a jet engine or something."

"Was it from one of the other science stations?" Ben said.

"Definitely too high performance for a foundation budget. It did have a logo on the door—a stylized red wolf."

Ben picked up Joe's tiny helmet and handed it to Ozzy.

"Who would do this to us?"

"I dunno, but I bet whoever's signing their paychecks had something to do with that antique nuclear reactor."

Ozzy set G.I. Joe on a shelf, put on a headset, and headed for the door. "I'm gonna see if I can get the power back on."

Cursed Curds

Out on the ice, Ozzy scanned the ruins of Earthwatch One. He trudged through the charred debris, and tried to get his bearings. He picked up a scorched lever from an office chair and scratched a diagram of the compound in the ice.

Okay, the ice-core storage vault was over there, and the Sno-Cat garage was right behind it, so the generator and fuel tank has to be over there.

Ozzy turned toward the only section of the steel-reinforced foundation wall still standing.

That's one badass wall. Maybe it shielded the generator from the blast.

Ozzy trudged through blackened snow toward the blast-pocked masonry. The stench of atomized building materials made his eyes water and his throat burn. Plodding through the smoking guts of his lab brought a wave of nausea that actual intestines never had. As he pressed on, it was obvious the wall wasn't as unscathed as it appeared from a distance. Several breaches in the concrete revealed the rebar within, giving the wall the appearance of a small-town jail in the old west.

If that generator didn't survive, neither will we.

Ozzy jogged the last few yards and bounded around the perimeter of the wall. Superficial dents and gouges scarred the insulated steel housing of the generator, but it looked sound. He pried open the warped access door.

Okay, okay, this looks good. Not a scratch. The conduits all look fine. So, what's the problem? Aha.

Ozzy toggled a tripped circuit breaker and the generator sputtered to life.

Ozzy adjusted his headset mic. "You got juice?"

"That's affirmative." Ben's reply crackled in his headset.

Ozzy inspected some pipes rising from the ice near a demolished domed structure. "The fuel tanks look all right."

He pried open a utility box, prodded the scorched electronics inside and pushed a fallen satellite dish back into position. "The VSAT's pretty toasty. Epic fail on the modems. No tweets for the peeps tonight. The dish looks okay, though."

Ozzy rummaged through the rubble in a decimated storeroom and found dozens of cardboard boxes. "Found some grub." The stenciled labels on the boxes read: TOFU. "To-fucking-fu."

"Excellent," Ben said.

Ozzy double-checked all the boxes.

They're all dehydrated tofu.

Ozzy searched the wreckage in a panic.

Where's my fucking food?

He scoured the debris and found a damaged satellite radio. Something shiny and brown glinted behind a scorched computer monitor.

Wait a minute.

Ozzy lunged at the shattered monitor and pushed it aside. A twin pack of Hostess cupcakes lay nestled in a drift of smoking debris and snow.

Yes.

Ozzy slipped them into his pocket and grabbed the radio.

As Ozzy made his way through the frozen ruins back to the Pit, he felt like an archeologist exploring the remnants of a lost civilization. Once familiar and useful objects filled him with an overwhelming sadness that bordered on dread. Ozzy stooped down and lifted a headless, Lenny Kravitz bobblehead from a drift of singed computer printouts. Terra gave it to him as a joke. Ozzy kicked the pile of papers.

Sorry, Lenny, your head's not in there. Terra couldn't say I'd look like you if I lost some weight if she could see you now.

Ozzy flicked the spring that protruded from Lenny's shoulders. It boinged a single, dissonant note, like the last note of a guitar solo dirge. Ozzy dropped the resin rock star and trudged on, but he couldn't shake the feeling he was being watched. He paused and listened, peering into the distance beyond the debris field. A faint screech seemed to hitch a ride on the gentle breeze that whistled through the mutilated architecture of Earthwatch One. Ozzy scrutinized the devastation that surrounded him.

What the fuck was that?

If he didn't know better, Ozzy might have dismissed the screech as the familiar call of a red-tailed hawk, common to the canyons he loved to hike, back in the world.

No hawks this far south. Too smart for that. Smarter than me, for sure.

Ozzy squinted and scrunched his nose. The mysterious screech brought a friend. A noxious stench wafted on the frigid breeze.

There's that gross fucking smell like back in the lab.

The closest Ozzy came to identifying the vile odor was picturing a bucket full of cigar butts that had been percolating in a marinade of vinegar and rotten shrimp.

As a man of science, Ozzy wasn't superstitious, but he hated mysterious shit, and he had more than his fill of mystery for one day. He hustled back to the Pit. He also wasn't easily spooked, but after all that had happened, the cavernous entrance to the stairwell resembled the gaping mouth of a tomb.

Ozzy descended the icy stairs, with caution, as he lugged the last two boxes of tofu back to the Pit. Even a minor injury could be the difference between survival and a lingering death.

He hip-bumped the heavy door open.

Inside, Ben Eaton studied the stacks of tofu boxes and wrote out a math problem in the air with his finger. "There's enough high-quality vegetable protein here to last several months." He ripped one of the boxes open and dumped the pasty cubes into a pot of boiling water.

"Bean slime blows," Ozzy said.

"You'll be eating healthy for a change."

Ozzy removed the cupcakes from his pocket with a flourish. "No tofu for me tonight, thanks." He sniffed them. "Ahhhh, sweet ambrosia."

"Those things are full of empty calories, preservatives and—"

"Flavor?"

Ben plopped some quivering cubes on a small plate and poured milky cooking water into a coffee mug.

"You're not going to drink that scum?" Ozzy said.

"It contains vital nutrients that were lost in cooking."

Ozzy removed a cupcake from its packaging while Ben nibbled tofu and sipped the cloudy water.

Ozzy raised a cupcake to his lips and taunted Ben. "As an appetizer, I lick the white squiggle that rests gently on a smooth layer of velvety fudge." Ozzy's tongue swept across the squiggles. He took a bite. "Below, the moist devils-food yields to my advances—until it surrenders the sweet secrets of its creamy center." Ozzy cupped it lovingly. He probed the airy cream with his tongue, flicking it lewdly at Ben. He wolfed it down and then the other.

"Do you think any of the other science stations know what happened to us?" Ben said.

"Not likely, they're way too far away," Ozzy said, as he licked chocolate off the packaging.

Ben sipped his tofu water, pious as a monk, and righteously indignant. With a belly full of bean curds, he got up and tinkered with the broken radio. "I don't believe we can receive, but I'm fairly certain we can send."

"How'll we know if you got through?'

"If we get rescued." Ben put on earphones and talked into the microphone. "Mayday, mayday, this is Earthwatch One. Do you read me?"

After hours of Ben's unanswered pleading, Ozzy fell asleep.

Solar Static

Ingrid scanned the far ice as she steered a Sno-Cat over the treacherous polar terrain.

This is going to be the day. I can feel it.

Her partner, Elsa, squinted at the GPS screen and said, "Looks like we're almost there. Let's find that monster crevasse before it finds us."

"No sign of it yet," Ingrid said.

Their radio crackled with heavy static. Ingrid strained to hear a faint voice as she fiddled with the knobs.

"Mayday, mayday. Do you read me? Anybody, this is Earthwatch One."

Damn. I don't need this, now of all days, but he sounds messed up.

Ingrid leaned toward the radio microphone. "We read you Earthwatch One. This is Ingrid Lindstrum."

Elsa added, "And Elsa Hedman, Swedish research station, Wasa, Queen Maud Land."

"We are about ten klicks north east of your station. Do you read me? Over," Ingrid said.

Static.

"Do you read me Earthwatch One?

Static.

"Copy this Earthwatch One, Solar flares are causing severe signal loss. Try another frequency."

"We're getting G-fours and fives out here," Elsa said. "Put on a pot of coffee. We're on our way. Do you copy Earthwatch One?"

No reply, only static.

Elsa turned down the volume on the radio down and grabbed the binoculars on the seat next to her. "I think I see the crevasse, Ingrid." She handed Ingrid the binoculars.

Their Sno-Cat lumbered to a stop.

Ingrid steadied the binoculars on the steering wheel, "Ja, ja, it's the big one all right. Turn off the GPS."

"Why?" Elsa said, "No one could find us if we—"

"Exactly. I don't want anyone to know where we are," Ingrid said, "I intend to be the first to publish this in the *Journal of Environmental Sciences*." She slammed the Sno-Cat into gear, "I can get us a little closer."

"We're close enough. This could be the beginning of a catastrophic collapse."

Ingrid nodded, handed the binoculars back to Elsa and said, "Meltwater production in the shear zone has doubled since last season."

"We should deploy the UAV," said Elsa.

"By *we*, you mean *me*. You deploy the drone this time. I've been driving for three hours."

"If I go out there, then I get to fly it, right?"

Ingrid zipped her parka and cinched the hood, "After what happened last time. I don't think so."

I appreciate her enthusiasm, but flying our UAV down into that crevasse, and crashing it, was reckless, and expensive."

"That wasn't my fault. It was really windy," Elsa said.

"Okay, I'll deploy the drone, but I'm flying it. You can set it up."

Ingrid smiled as Elsa lifted the state-of-the-art quadcopter from its sturdy case, attached the high-res camera to the gimbal, and snapped in the battery.

"Is the battery hot?"

Elsa handed her the drone, "Yeah, but you only have five minutes, tops, before it freezes."

Ingrid backed out the door and positioned the drone on the frost-covered hood of the Sno-Cat.

Elsa slid into the driver-side of the bench seat, switched the controller on, and adjusted the monitor.

Ingrid hustled back inside.

Elsa passed her the controller. Their eyes locked for a little too long and Elsa's cheeks flushed. She couldn't have looked more like Snow White if she'd been holding a poison apple.

Ingrid yanked off her gloves, threw back the hood of her parka, and positioned the controller on her lap. Her Norse features and determined expression seemed fitting for such cold and dangerous place. She rubbed her hands together, and wiggled her fingers with the flair of a concert pianist.

Elsa laughed.

Ingrid said, "What?"

Elsa cocked her head and beamed. "I love it when you do that."

"What?"

"That thing with your fingers."

Ingrid smiled, "Well, I love it when you laugh."

If Elsa didn't have a husband back in Stockholm, Ingrid could imagine they might have been more than colleagues.

Ingrid worked the joysticks with the agility of a twelve-year-old gamer on a boss run.

Elsa said, "Warp factor one, Mr. Sulu."

Ingrid socked her in the arm and said, "That was funny the first time you said it."

The drone's quad props hummed to life. The dragonfly rose from the Sno-Cat's hood, hovered, and sped out of sight.

Ingrid and Elsa watched the monitor as the drone soared into the cold blue yonder—one, two, three, four hundred feet above the alabaster icescape.

Ingrid's eyes widened as she leaned in closer to the flickering screen, "Are you getting this?"

Elsa said, "You betcha, full HD, 1080p—12 mega pixels."

"I thought there was only going to be one giant crevasse," Ingrid said, "There are hundreds of them."

"Look at the meltwater draining into all those surface crevasses."

A layman would marvel at this wonder of nature, but I feel like I have a front row seat for the end of the world.

"When that water freezes, they'll be like wedges and cause a catastrophic calving like we've never seen before," Ingrid said

"Bigger than the Larsen C shelf collapse?"

"Much bigger."

Ingrid stared into the monitor. For a moment, she thought the screen had shattered. A web of colossal crevasses stretched for miles in all directions.

Elsa's already big eyes widened and her rosebud lips tensed. "When will the ice shelf calve?"

"Not until all the meltwater freezes—sometime next winter," Ingrid said.

"Damn, we'll be back in Sweden by then."

"Trust me, you don't want to be around when this shelf collapses."

Elsa looked at her watch, "Shit, it's been almost five minutes. Better bring the drone back before the battery freezes."

Seconds later, the drone touched down on the hood of the Sno-Cat.

Elsa shrugged, "Never mind."

Ingrid switched off the controller and said, "Punch in the coordinates for Earthwatch One."

So, So Small

Ozzy awoke to the sound of grunting.

Ben screwed on the back cover of the television. "I fixed it."

Ozzy sat up in his cot. "Great, you got the radio working."

Hope they have hot cocoa on the rescue chopper.

"No, the television," Ben said and turned it on. The Sony logo flashed on the massive screen followed by a series of grunts and groans as Jason Statham pummeled five or six fools who pissed him off.

Ozzy grabbed the remote, zapped the TV off and said, "We don't have time for this shit." He laced up his boots. "We're going topside."

He doesn't fucking get it. It's survival time and that means holding up and holding on until help comes.

"Is that wise? I mean, what if those bad guys are still lurking around?"

Ozzy couldn't tell if it was a bead of sweat or a tear Ben wiped away with the back of his trembling hand. Ozzy wanted to be sympathetic, but Ben had wimped-out so often that any compassion he once felt for his friend had turned to exasperation.

"We need to see what we can salvage."

"Perhaps I should stay here and work on the radio."

"Negatory. You're comin' with me."

Ozzy laced up his snow boots with one eye on Eaton who sorted through his thermal turtlenecks like a clerk at a sporting goods store.

"Are you serious?" Ozzy said, "Wear the blue one."

"The red one is warmer, but it's rather scratchy."

"Quit stalling and get dressed."

Eaton suited up in slow motion.

Ozzy stood by the door with his arms folded.

Stall all you want. You're not getting out of going out on the ice by playing the skinny card. Not this time.

"I know what you're doing, Ben."

"What?" Ben looked at Ozzy with innocent eyes.

"What you always do. Wait until I get so frustrated with your silly-ass tactics that I go out on the ice by myself."

"I do no such thing."

"C'mon."

"I'll have you know that I have valid concerns when it comes to certain aspects of our mission."

"Oh, you mean the hard work part."

"No, the cold part. It is freezing out there. Subzero, to be precise."

"Ya think?"

"If I freeze to death up there, you will be guilty of negligent homicide."

"If you don't lace those boots up in the next thirty seconds, I'll be guilty of murder one."

Ozzy stifled a grin as Ben laced his boots like his life depended on it.

I probably should have gone out on my own as usual. He's going to make me regret taking him with me. I just know it.

Ozzy yanked open the heavy, insulated door.

Cold air rushed in.

Ben trotted out without making eye contact.

Ozzy pulled the door shut behind him.

Ben climbed the icy stairs like they were steps to a gallows. As Ben neared the bright rectangle of light at the top of the stairwell, Ozzy had a revelation.

Fuck, Ben hasn't seen our science station blown to shit yet.

Ozzy hustled up the last few steps so his friend wouldn't have to witness the devastation alone.

Ben stood motionless amid the rubble. Down in the Pit, Ben's irksome personality filled the confined space from floor to ceiling with his annoying quirks and oddball opinions, but out on the endless ice, he seemed so, so small.

For the first time ever, Ozzy felt small too. He rested a hand on Ben's shoulder, and they stared out at their smoldering science station without saying a word. The blackened ruins were the embodiment of desolation and isolation. The wind had polished the sky a chilling lapis blue.

Even though Ben was right next to him, Ozzy never felt so alone. His sense of purpose and security had been incinerated like the debris that surrounded him. Only the primal compulsion for survival remained. Defining and achieving goals always came easy for Ozzy, but simply staying alive had never been one of his goals before. The skill set that facilitated his academic and professional success seemed irrelevant now. At least his months in the Antarctic made him ice-savvy. It was a good start, and it gave him confidence in his endurance, but he knew that wouldn't be nearly enough.

Ben's shoulder trembled.

Ozzy sensed it wasn't from the cold.

I should have come alone. He doesn't have the beans for this.

Ozzy said, "We'll get through this, buddy."

Ben rested his head on Ozzy's shoulder. "Do you really think so?"

"Sure. No worries. This is as bad as it could possibly get, and we got through it without a scratch."

Ben pointed to the kindling that once was their lab. "What about our research? The computers, the equipment, they are all gone."

"I back-up our data to the cloud every day. Everything else is just stuff, heavily insured stuff."

"I feel much better already."

"Okay, then. Let's do this. The food isn't going to find itself."

Foraging for Food

Ozzy slogged through the rubble toward the storage shed's last known location.

It has to be around here someplace.

When Ozzy kicked a pile of carbonized toiletries, he hit pay dirt. Darth Vader leered at him from the label of a *Star Wars* gummy vitamin bottle. It was one of three that were fused together in a tangle of melted toothbrushes. They had never been opened, and the plastic bottles were only slightly warped from the heat. Ozzy pried them loose from a colorful nest of serpentine toothbrush handles and stuffed them in his pockets.

A few feet ahead, several family-size cans of beef stew huddled together beside what looked like a postmodern sculpture. Ozzy wandered over for a closer look. Upon closer inspection, the sculpture was a stainless-steel examination table bent at odd angles by the explosion. Ozzy snatched up an electrical screwdriver next to the post-modern masterpiece.

There you are. I've been looking everywhere for you.

Ozzy used it to pry one of the large cans from a brown, stewy concretion of gravy, meat, and vegetables. He tossed the damaged can aside and checked out the others. They all had been ruptured by the blast. For a moment, Ozzy thought he could salvage the stew since it was frozen, but fiberglass insulation ruined the recipe. What Ozzy really needed to find now was hope, but he didn't have any idea where to even begin looking for that.

As Ozzy searched through drifts of charred rubble for more provisions, a rustling sound rose up from behind a twisted wall module.

Ozzy crept closer.

The big, black eyes of a fuzzy seal pup stared up at him. Ozzy's reflection shimmered in their onyx translucence, and despite his growing sense of dread, he smiled.

The pup yelped as Ozzy picked him up.

"Yeah, yeah, you're cute and you know it."

Ben waved from a few yards away. "Hey Ozzy, I found something."

Ozzy trudged toward his partner and yet another gutted seal.

He covered the pup's eyes.

Ben prodded the carcass with a shard of plexiglass. "This one's still warm."

Ozzy held up the pup. "*This* one's alive."

The wriggling ball of fur squeaked like a cuddly, stuffed animal.

As they surveyed the carnage, a *screech* sounded from several yards away.

"What was that?" Ben said.

"Don't know. I heard it yesterday, but that was much closer."

Ben sniffed the air, "And that nauseating odor. It smells like—"

"Trouble. Let's go below."

Screech.

Ozzy spun around.

Two red eyes glimmered in the shadows of a ruptured 55-gallon drum.

Screech.

High above, three silhouettes peered down from their perch on a twisted iron beam.

A cacophony of *screeching* cut through the katabatic wind.

Ozzy and Ben whipped around.

Hundreds of penguins waddled toward them from fifty yards beyond the debris-field.

A wild-eyed penguin leaped from the 55-gallon drum. It clanged like an alarm bell as the wind pushed the drum aside on the uneven ice. The penguin charged Ozzy with surprising speed, with its head thrust forward and flippers swept back.

What's an aquatic bird doing so far inland?

Ozzy moved toward the penguin as it advanced on him. As it closed the gap between them, he got a closer look at the creature.

You're one fucking ugly penguin.

The creature leaped at Ozzy's face, feet first, with its enormous talons splayed for attack. Ozzy tucked the seal pup under one arm and deflected the airborne assault with the other. The powerful sweep of his forearm sent the brutish bird crashing to the ice. It slid and rolled, for several yards, but renewed its attack from below. Its oversized beak snapped with mindless rapidity, as it glared at Ozzy with malevolent determination. Ozzy clutched the seal pup like a quarterback clutching a fluffy football as he maneuvered out of the way of the monster's charge. With a classic sidestep fake-out, the creature zoomed right past Ozzy.

Okay, you're fast and nasty, but you still have a bird brain.

The creature slid to a stop and pivoted for another pass. It looked like no animal Ozzy had ever seen, with its cranial fin, deep-set eyes, huge talons, and sharp bone spurs on the end of its flippers. It had burly, upper-body musculature that was totally un-avian. As monstrous as the brute looked, it smelled even worse. Unlike the sub-zero temperature, the sight and stink of the hideous thing gave Ozzy a chill.

You're no ordinary penguin if you're a penguin at all.

The creature attacked again, but when Ozzy repeated his fake-out, the little monster anticipated the maneuver and ripped Ozzy's leg open with one, sure snap. For a split second, Ozzy felt nothing, but when blood spurted from the rip in his snow-pants, he felt plenty.

Mother fucker.

He throttled the crazed bird and punted it into a pile of shattered windowpanes and split timber.

A penguin with tentacles protruding from tumorous

lesions below its snapping beak attacked Ozzy from behind. Its serpentine appendages wrapped around his knee and slithered up his inner thigh.

Ozzy whipped around as the creature pinned his thigh with its sharp, flipper spurs, snapping and snipping, as it tentacles constricted tighter and tighter. Ozzy wailed and fumbled in his pocket for the screwdriver, never loosening his grip on the whimpering pup. He got a good grip on the screwdriver and thrust it into the monster's eye until he hit bone, but it just kept ripping into his leg. Bone cracked and popped when Ozzy drove the shaft all the way to the handle. The tentacles loosened their grip. The creature slid down Ozzy's bloody leg and convulsed on the ice at his feet. Ozzy stomped the avian abomination. The little monster screeched.

The advancing horde screeched in reply.

Ozzy continued stomping long after the creature was dead, as if pulverizing the hideous thing might purge the sight of it from his memory.

Ben scurried up a lattice of mangled rebar as mutant penguins snapped at his heels.

Ozzy sidestepped the waddling monstrosities. "Ben, get the hell outta here."

Ben dodged the mutants all the way to the stairwell.

The seal pup squirmed out of Ozzy's arms and charged the advancing little terrors.

Come back here, you. I couldn't take it, if anything happened to you.

Ozzy took off after the yipping little fur ball and snatched it up as the mutants converged.

A huge bull seal barked as he charged from behind a collapsed retaining wall.

Ozzy slid the pup over to him and they scuttled away to safety.

Hey, your dad came back for you, and he looks pissed. Later, little guy.

The mutants redirected their attention on Ozzy as he dashed for the stairwell.

A gauntlet of razor-sharp beaks blocked his retreat.

He kicked a path through the snapping mutant legion.

They slashed through his pants and tore into the meat inside. Wisps of vapor, from the open wounds, trailed behind Ozzy as he pushed forward. His blood-soaked pants had already frozen stiff, and it was getting harder and harder to bend his knees.

A muscular albino penguin blocked his path to the stairwell. It towered above the rest. The beast let out a high-pitched shriek.

Ozzy stopped in his bloody tracks and covered his ears.

The mutant swarm halted and fell silent.

Ozzy and the creature faced off. Their eyes locked. Ozzy's heart pounded.

"Never seen anything like me before? Well, I never saw anything like you."

The freakish albino took a step forward.

If I back up he'll be on me in a second.

Ozzy stepped forward too.

"Well, tekeli-fucking-li. You picked the wrong day to fuck with me, you Lovecraftian lookin' motherfucker."

Ozzy grabbed a broken piece of pipe.

The albino lunged.

Ozzy swung through and delivered a crushing blow.

The creature tumbled down the stairs.

Ozzy followed.

The beast thrashed on the landing and sunk its beak into Ozzy's ankle. The meat pain in his legs was immediately superseded by searing bone pain.

Ozzy burst through the door, dragging the albino behind him.

Ben reeled backward.

Ozzy slammed the steel door shut, decapitating the alabaster brute.

The maniacal bird's head tumbled, still snapping, across the floor.

"Are you all right?" Ben said.

Ozzy flopped down on his cot and peeked inside the bloody rips on his pants. "Shit."

"Let me take a look at that," Ben said, and grabbed a medical kit from some industrial shelving. He popped the lid and piled medical supplies on Ozzy's lap.

Ben slipped on purple latex gloves and grabbed a pair of surgical scissors.

Ozzy squirmed. "Time out. Put all that sharp shit back into your little box of horrors. Just bandage my leg and be done with it."

"Not so fast. You can be so infantile, sometimes."

Ozzy closed his eyes as Ben snipped the pant legs open.

Ben said, "I can't believe penguins would do something like this."

"Those were *not* normal penguins. I sure as shit didn't see any happy feet up there." Ozzy howled when Ben squeezed antiseptic on his wounds. He opened his eyes. "Why not rub some salt on it, while you're at it?"

"That will not be necessary. This Betadine is more than adequate. Although, in ancient times, salt would have been the antiseptic of choice."

"This hurts like a motherfucker, Ben, and you're making it worse."

"I can fix that," Ben said, as he filled a syringe from a small bottle.

"The only thing I hate worse that sharp shit is pointy shit. I don't consent to this medical procedure."

"A little morphine will reduce your pain, in no time."

Ozzy folded his arms and said, "Good luck trying to shoot me up with that."

Ben plunged the syringe into Ozzy's thigh, and injected the morphine."

Ozzy yelped. "I thought you had to stick it in my arm."

"I gave you a subcutaneous intramuscular injection. It will take a little longer to kick in, but it will help."

"If you wanna help," Ozzy said, "Put that sharp shit away and... whoa, it helps."

Ben unwrapped a large suture needle.

"Oh, hell no," Ozzy said, "Get that fish hook away from me."

"Most of these wounds are too large. I have to close them. See for yourself."

Ozzy squinted and took a quick glance at his leg. Clumps of pink fat protruded from the larger gashes.

"Okay, okay, sew me up, but make it snappy."

Ben poked a fatty glob back in and sutured the wound.

Ozzy squirmed. Ben stuck himself with the suture needle. "Ouch. Stop fidgeting."

"How bad is it?"

"The wounds are superficial." Ben squeezed a glob of fat. "Although, you may die at any time of coronary artery disease from all this blubber."

"Those thing's beaks are razor fucking sharp."

"There's more going on here than a few isolated mutations," Ben said, "it seems more like—"

"Accelerated evolution?"

"More like de-evolution."

"What, penguisauruses?" Ozzy said, "If the lab wasn't blown to shit, I'd sequence the DNA from the albino's head and—"

"How can we possibly deal with creatures like that?" Ben said, as he tied off the last stitch.

"We have to find a way outta here. Like, *now*," Ozzy said.

"No, no, no, this is like *Night of the Living Dead*. The obnoxious bald man was correct all along. The Pit is like the basement. We wait here until help comes."

"We gotta go, Ben," Ozzy pointed to the door, "This is no zombie movie."

"I wouldn't last long out on the ice. I don't have the subcutaneous fat you have," Ben said, trying to look as pitiful as possible.

"Okay, you stay and I'll go for help."

"You can't go out there. Look what those things did to you."

"I have to at least give it a try." Ozzy stood up and stumbled toward the door.

I feel like shit.

"Don't leave me here alone, Ozzy. Please."

He's as helpless as that baby seal, but not half as brave.

"Okay, okay, but just until I feel better. I'm not waiting around here forever."

Ben gathered up the medical waste like a tip-stiffed waiter bussing a table. He opened an access door in the wall and pitched the bloody trash in a chute. He flicked a switch. Hungry metal blades ground madly.

Rescue RSVP

Ingrid Lindstrum hunched over the steering wheel of her Sno-Cat as if six inches closer to the windshield would afford her a clearer view of the ice ahead. A gnawing sense of dread radiated from the base of her spine as she and Elsa neared Earthwatch One. A mayday at the bottom of the world was unnerving enough without the possibility of a catastrophic ice shelf collapse. Her nerves were rattled, and she was afraid she couldn't hide it much longer. It wasn't cold inside the heated cab, but that didn't keep Ingrid from shaking ever so slightly.

Elsa rested her hand on Ingrid's knee, "Hey, you okay?"

Ingrid forced a smile, "Yeah, yeah, I'm good. Long day at the office that's all."

The diesel engines of the Sno-Cat were noisy, but Ingrid was sure she heard an ominous screeching sound off in the distance. She studied Elsa's face for any hint she might have heard it too, but she just looked bored and a little tired.

Ingrid maneuvered the Sno-Cat through a maze of towering ice spires, and then she saw it, the smoldering ruins of Earthwatch One. The blackened debris-field resembled an abstract mandala hovering in an endless expanse of stark white oblivion.

"What the hell happened here?" Ingrid said.

"Some kind of explosion. Gas leak?" Elsa said.

"I don't know. That's a lot of damage."

"There could be injuries."

"I'm calling this in. We're pretty far from base." Ingrid switched the VSAT on.

Static.

"Damn solar flares," Elsa said.

Ingrid handed the mic to Elsa. "Keep trying."

As they neared the charred wreckage of Ozzy's Sno-Cat, a chorus of frantic chirps and peeps filled the cab.

"Is the radio making that sound?" Ingrid said.

Elsa switched the VSAT off. "No, it's coming from over there." She pointed to Ozzy's torched Sno-Cat.

Ingrid stopped and rolled down her window. "What do you think it is?" Elsa's eyes widened like a kid in a spook house. "Maybe somebody is trapped in there. I'll check it out."

If someone is hurt, I don't know what we can do about it. We don't even have a first aid kit.

Elsa climbed down and trudged over to Ozzy's Sno-Cat. She peered inside the burned-out interior of the cab.

Wish I could be more like Elsa, she's always so eager to help, no matter what it is she's doing. I just want to get back to base and drink a glass of akvavit in front of the fire.

"Ingrid, take a look at this," Elsa called out.

Ingrid climbed out of the warm cab and hurried over to Elsa.

Dozens of penguin chicks shivered inside the scorched interior of Ozzy's Sno-Cat. Their red, pleading eyes stared up at Ingrid.

Ingrid looked around and said, "Where's their mother?"

"We can't just let them freeze in there," Elsa said.

"She's probably scavenging food," said Ingrid as she pointed to the Sno-Cat. "She'll be back. Let's go."

"But they're so cute—and helpless." Elsa unzipped her parka and stuffed the fuzzy chicks inside.

Ingrid said, "Stop. If your scent gets on them, their mother will abandon them for sure."

Elsa squirmed and laughed as she continued stuffing the wiggly chicks inside her parka. "That tickles," she said, "They're so cuddly."

Ingrid stepped closer to Elsa. "Okay, play time is over. Put those penguins back and—"

Elsa's eyes widened. Her mouth gaped. She screamed. A

wet, red circle radiated, ever wider, in the front of her parka. She stumbled in awkward circles, dropped to her knees, and flailed on the red ice.

Ingrid rushed to her side and unzipped Elsa's parka in time to see a chick wriggle into a jagged hole in Elsa's belly, and disappear.

Ingrid recoiled, then without thinking, plunged her hand into her friend's abdomen. She grabbed the tiny monster by its flaying webbed feet and yanked it out.

The blood-soaked nestling gulped a plum-colored morsel of organ meat as Elsa's frantic screams gave way to throaty groans and infantile whimpers.

Ingrid flung the slippery thing over her shoulder, but not before several more of the hellish chicks had squirmed inside the steaming cavity in her partner's abdomen.

The sound of chattering beaks and the slosh of minced entrails filled Ingrid with a terror that would have left her paralyzed if not for a primal rage that drove her to action. She plunged both hands into the roiling mass of bloated mutants. Their tiny bones shattered in Ingrid's merciless grip, but Elsa no longer thrashed in pain.

For a moment, Ingrid thought she saw Elsa move, but it was the mutant chicks making a meal of her friend, from inside her shredded parka.

Ingrid throttled a snapping runt, as it nudged its siblings aside for a turn at the sweet, hot meat. One glance at Elsa's face snuffed out all hope that she was still alive. Her frost white eyes, frozen in dire surprise, stared out at nothing. Ice crystals glistened on Elsa's too blue lips, stretched taught over a gaping mouth that once laughed and kissed and ranted about climate politics.

Ingrid felt alone in a way she never had before. She knew what it felt like to be lonely, but this was different. Loneliness was like hunger, a simple drive that needed to be satisfied. Back home, she could always call a friend or walk to the corner bar, but this frozen emptiness that spread out in all directions mocked her with a desperate sense of isolation.

The fact that Elsa was dead only intensified Ingrid's resolve to crush the life out of the hideous imps, but the snipping, snapping mutant spawn ripped through her gloves and turned her hands into raw meat in an instant.

Ingrid screamed—the kind of scream that might be mistaken for laughter.

Ingrid stumbled to her Sno-Cat. She knew that if she looked at her hands, she might pass out before she reached the safety of her Sno-Cat. The harder her heart pounded, the more her hands hurt. She kept her eyes on her boots and the ice ahead. The cold, dry wind swept away the wisps of steam rising with each scarlet pulse.

As Ingrid reached the cab, she looked back. Most of what remained of her life pooled behind her in the snow. Her face ached from tears, frozen solid on her cheeks. She would have whisked them away, but that would have required more dexterity than she could muster.

She tried to pull herself into the driver's seat by grabbing the gearshift, but her hands were done grabbing things.

The Sno-Cat popped into gear and lurched forward.

Ingrid tumbled from the cab and onto the snow like a sailor swept overboard with no land in sight.

As her life dribbled out one heart-pulse at a time, her Sno-Cat pull away like a ghost-ship—adrift on an endless sea of ice.

Tentacles & Tofu

Down in the Pit, Ben plopped soggy tofu on a plate and handed it to Ozzy. He stabbed a quivering cube with a fork and took a tiny bite. "This crap doesn't taste *that* bad. In fact, it doesn't have much taste at all."

"That-a-boy."

Ozzy shivered. "But, man-o-man, the *texture's* a bitch."

Ozzy swallowed the soppy cubes like bitter pills.

Ben tried to stifle a grin.

I have to get that taste out of my mouth.

"Would you like a *Star Wars* vitamin, they're gummy?" Ozzy said as he flipped the lid on the jar.

"Surely you jest. Your so-called vitamins contain gelatin derived from animal collagen. I wouldn't be surprised if those vile things were loaded with sugar.

"Suit yourself." Ozzy said as he popped a cherry flavored Darth Maul in his mouth, limped to the bathroom, and paused at the door. "If you're so fucking healthy, why do you look so anemic?"

Inside the bathroom, Ozzy screwed in a bare bulb that dangled overhead. He opened the medicine cabinet, grabbed a crusty toothbrush, and turned on the faucet. Rusty water swirled in the sink.

Salsa music boomed outside the bathroom door. Ozzy peeked through a crack.

On the television, a hot Latina shimmied to a big musical number on a Spanish language variety show.

Ben did the forbidden dance with his pillow.

Ozzy wandered in from the bathroom.

Ben stopped mid-pillow-hump. They both laughed.

Bang, bang, bang. The door quaked. They both jumped back.

"Penguins?" Ben said.

"How's a penguin gonna pound on a door?"

"I don't know. What then?"

"A Jehovah's Witness? How the fuck should I know?"

"What do we do now?"

Ozzy inched toward the door. "I dunno, what do *you* wanna do?"

Ben clutched his pillow like a teddy bear. "Something. We have to do *something.*"

Ozzy pressed his ear to the door. *Bang, bang, bang.* He sprang backward like a startled cat and shouted, "Who the hell goes there?"

Something that sounded like muffled screams came from outside.

Ben clutched his pillow even tighter. "What on earth was that?"

"Want me to open the door and find out?" Ozzy glared at Ben with a look he hoped exuded more frustration than a letter to the editor.

"No, no, no—don't do that!"

"It's probably just the wind blowing the storage drum around the stairwell."

"What if it's Roland with all his tourists?" Ben said.

Ozzy waved the idea away, "No way. Roland isn't coming for quite a while."

Ozzy stood for a minute eyeing the door with suspicion. He eased himself onto a wooden folding chair. It creaked as he squirmed to get comfortable. He grabbed the remote.

"What do you intend to do now?" Ben said.

"What I always do when I don't know what to do." Ozzy zapped through the channels with a vengeance.

Ozzy and Ben settled down and watched a tabloid talk show, but Ben had his eyes on the door more than the television.

On screen, a middle-aged couple held hands. The husband

wore nothing but a huge diaper and a floppy bonnet. The host shoved a microphone in the man-child's face. "Honey, all I really want is for you to change my doodoo pants." The big baby's wife grimaced and leaned away.

"Most of these talk show people are ringers," Ben said.

Ozzy shrugged, zapped through the channels and stopped on another talk show. The host interviewed a withered old crone. She looked like a prostitute granny as she pulled up her droopy fishnet stockings. She adjusted her baggy lingerie and said, "You try living on Social Security."

"Actress. Seen her on the soaps," Ben said.

"Do you mind?" Ozzy said.

Ozzy thought he heard a faint scratching sound coming from the airshaft. He scrutinized the ceiling register, saw nothing and continued watching the show.

The crotchety hooker fussed with her cheap blue wig, "You think I *like* servicing grunting old gummers?" She wagged her finger at the host and continued, "Do you have any idea how hard it is to wash off the old man smell?"

The scratching in the shaft grew louder amid the old woman's chatter. "At least I have Spaghetti-O's in the cupboard."

Ben said, "How can you watch this moronic, misogynistic charade?"

The scratching in the airshaft turned into loud, metallic thumps.

Ozzy turned his attention to the ceiling register, just in time to see it fall on top of a metal bookcase—with one of the mutants close behind.

Ozzy sat at attention. "What the—"

The mutant leaped from the shelf to the television then onto Ozzy's lap. "Fuck?"

Ozzy tumbled backward on his folding chair, rolled head over heels and landed on his belly.

Ben leaped from his chair, rushed over to Ozzy and rolled him over.

Ozzy struggled to his feet. A squashed mutant lay dead on the floor.

Ben poked the flattened intruder with his foot—it was dead.

Screech.

Ben and Ozzy both whipped around. Fleshy spaghetti tentacles dangled from the airshaft, followed by the finned head of another mutant. It wriggled out and hopped from the shelf to the floor.

Yet another screeching monstrosity squirmed out.

One leaped at Ozzy; the other at Ben.

Ozzy fought off his attacker with a mop.

Ben kept his mutant at bay with a folding chair.

Ozzy pinned the snapping freak with the mop and snapped its neck.

"There's no need for violence, Ozzy," Ben said, "If we can just make them understand we mean them no harm..."

The mutant wrapped its tentacles around the chair leg, snipped it off a like a breadstick, and lunged at Ben.

He screamed and smashed the intruder with the chair.

"I think it understood that," Ozzy said.

Screech.

Another mutant peered from the airshaft.

Ben pointed and whimpered.

Ozzy grabbed a knife, climbed the sturdy metal shelving, and jabbed at the black and white monstrosity. Its snapping beak was sharper than his blade, so Ozzy covered the opening of the shaft with a thick book from the shelf—Darwin's *The Origin of Species.*

"Cut the heating duct at both ends," Ozzy said as he tossed the knife to Ben.

"But—"

"*Hurry.*"

Ben climbed on a chair and cut the flexible, insulated duct.

As Ozzy struggled to hold the book in place, a beak gouged through the center.

"Gimme that damn duct," Ozzy said.

Ben complied.

Ozzy removed the book, and slid the duct over the opening of the shaft. "Quick, shove the other end in the trash grinder."

Ben opened the trash grinder door and stuffed the duct in the chute. The duct swelled with mutants.

"Shall I switch the grinder on?" Ben said.

"Abso-fucking-lutely."

Ben flicked the switch. The whole room vibrated from the gnashing, grinding, and screeching.

Ben stumbled over to Ozzy and gazed up.

Ozzy struggled to hold his end of the duct in place.

"Shall I fetch some duct tape?" Ben said.

"You're my idea man today, Ben."

Cryogenic Coldburn

Some Hours Later

Relentless pecking reverberated inside the cramped living quarters. Ozzy ignored the sound of mutants congregating in the stairwell.

Ben stared at the door. "Those horrible creatures are determined to get in here."

"Let 'em try. The door is three-eighths inch steel both sides with a six inch insulation core in between."

"They found a way in before."

"It's all fixed, now. I secured the airshaft with Metro shelving from the bookcase. I repaired the heating duct. What more do you want?"

"All that blood spattered around the trash grinder door. It's very disconcerting."

"So, clean it up. Can't you see I'm busy?" Ozzy didn't look up as he measured and marked a chunk of wood. He tossed it on a pile of dismantled folding chairs and parked the stubby pencil behind his ear. He grinned and released the lock on the tape measure. The steel ribbon of inches recoiled with a satisfying snap.

"You are ruining our chairs," Ben said.

"I left one for you."

"But they were a set."

"Expecting company?"

"I can't take it anymore."

"They're only chairs." Ozzy grabbed a saw from the cluster

of tools that surrounded him and ripped the blade across a dismembered chair leg.

"Not the chairs, the infernal pecking. Can't you do something to make them stop?"

"Like what?"

"I don't know. Shoot them with your guns or something." Ben pointed to a pair of guns mounted on the wall.

"You want me to shoot monsters with paintball guns?"

"We have a situation here."

Crackle beep.

"What was that?" Ben said.

Ozzy stopped sawing. What?

"That sound."

"I didn't hear anything."

"It came from over there." Ben pointed to the Metro shelving.

Crackle beep.

"There it is again." Ben pulled his knees to his chest.

"I know what it is," said Ozzy.

"Penguins?"

No, no, no." Ozzy put his saw down, and walked over to the shelving.

Crackle beep.

Ozzy brushed off sawdust from his snow pants, and picked up a device from the shelf.

Crackle beep

Ben hopped up and dashed over to Ozzy for a closer look.

"What on Earth is that?" Ben said.

"That's weird." Ozzy held the mini Geiger counter at arm's length, and swept the room. When he pointed it at the spot where he squashed the mutant, the beep crackled louder, and faster.

Ben looked over Ozzy's shoulder with alarm.

"Something in the Pit is radioactive," Ozzy said. The closer he got to the trash chute, the louder the Geiger counter squawked. "It's those damn penguins—they're hot."

"Have we been contaminated with radioactive material?" Ben said.

Ozzy handed Ben the device. "See for yourself."

Ben squinted at the digital display. "Sixty microSieverts."

"Less than a dental x-ray."

"Do you suppose radiation is causing normal penguins to mutate?"

"Sure. That portable reactor was hot as hell. If it weren't so damn cold, it probably would have melted down. Could be worse, though."

"What could possibly be worse?"

"Well, if this was like a 50s science fiction movie, those fuckers would be fifty feet tall."

"This isn't funny, Ozzy. It's an ecological disaster."

"You're right. I'm sorry. It's just that this whole thing is so fucking nuts."

"I regret not preserving one of those creatures for a thorough examination."

Ozzy pointed to the door and said, "Plenty more where they came from."

Ben shook his head and covered his ears to muffle the pecking. He sat back down on his folding chair and rocked like a devout penitent.

"Calm the fuck down, damn it. Just crank up the TV and relax."

Ben grabbed the remote and turned up the volume.

A candlelit boudoir flashed on the screen. A comely chambermaid pleasured a handsome squire on a Victorian bed.

"Now, this looks like something you would enjoy," Ben said.

Ozzy glanced up from his woodworking. "Pseudo-porn."

"Sex is sex."

"That's not sex. It's a simulation. That guy's sittin' on his limp dick."

"That's preposterous."

"No, look. Look at angle of her ass. He'd have to have a cock on his stomach unless it's two feet long."

Ozzy drilled holes in the wood as the chambermaid cried out in scripted ecstasy.

"They must be having intercourse," Ben said, "Look, she's having an orgasm."

Ozzy continued to screw pieces of wood together

I love it when a plan comes together. It won't be long now.

Ben zapped through the channels, "Anything you would like to watch?"

"No. I have work to do."

"What are you making?"

"You'll see, when it's done."

Zap-zap-zap

An ice-packed corpse lay on an operating table. A creepy looking documentary host leaned on the table, Rod Serling style, and said, "Cryonics, souls on ice. Dying may no longer be the death sentence it once was."

"This looks interesting," Ben said.

Gurgling fluids surged through clear tubing, tethered to the ashen cadaver by long embalming needles.

"Mr. Coldburn suffers from an inoperable brain tumor," the narrator said, "The Cryonova Corporation will replace his blood with glycerol to minimize cell damage when he's immersed in liquid nitrogen. He will remain in a state of cryo-stasis until a cure can be found."

Mr. Coldburn's icy countenance filled the screen.

"He's as dead as Tutankhamun," Ben said.

Medics wrapped Mr. Coldburn's body in Mylar.

Ozzy glanced up from his work, "Not necessarily."

"Oh, he's dead all right," Ben said.

The medics lowered Mr. Coldburn into a cylindrical chamber.

"They freeze 'em right before they take their last breath," Ozzy said.

"He was an ice sculpture when he hit the liquid nitrogen. It's minus 200 degrees centigrade."

"Remember the kid who fell through the ice on some frozen lake a few years ago? They brought him back after he was underwater for forty-five minutes."

"It's not the same thing."

"Forty-five minutes, forty-five years—twenty years ago, the kid woulda been dead in the water. Twenty years from now,

Walt Disney will open a theme-park on the Moon."

"Walt Disney wasn't frozen, but I suppose *you'd* like to be cryogenically preserved."

"No fucking way. Freezing blows, especially down here. When I die, I wanna rest in fucking peace."

"The dead always rest in peace, do they not?"

Ozzy paced with his screwdriver. "If you freeze down here, you may look dead, but you won't be dead-dead, not like some guy who gets hit by a bus in Chicago. You'll be suspended like Mr. what's-his-name in the tank."

"Coldburn, Mr. Coldburn."

"Like Mr. Coldburn, trapped inside a frozen body, thinking scary frozen thoughts, enduring the conscience awareness of the cold and the silence for billions of years—till the sun goes super nova and incinerates the entire fucking solar system. Can you wait that long to be warm again?"

"You're a lunatic, and I'm crazy for arguing with you."

"We'll see who's a lunatic when you're frozen solid in the sterile polar ice."

"And what if you should freeze, down here?"

"I'll envy the rotting dead."

"That's enough." Ben covered his ears.

"I'll envy the rotting dead in their lush green cemeteries, with their cozy rot, and their wiggly worms."

"I can't hear you."

Ozzy wagged his screwdriver at Ben. "Natural decomposition. That's what *I'm* into, Ben—the luxury of natural decomposition."

Ben pushed Ozzy's screwdriver out of his face. "Are you done creeping me out?"

Ozzy shrugged and went back to his woodworking project.

On TV, the creepy host dipped a rose in liquid nitrogen and tapped it on the side of the cylinder—it shattered.

Of Shrieking Skulls and Happy Trees

Days Later

Ozzy sat cross-legged in the La-Z-Boy he'd constructed from scrap wood and his *Star Wars* blanket. He scraped off the last few feathers and bits of desiccated flesh from the decapitated, albino penguin's skull with a pocketknife.

Should I donate you to the Smithsonian, when we get out of here, or keep you as a paperweight?

Ben tittered with delight as he watched TV.

Ozzy looked up from his defleshing.

He's so easily amused.

Ben sat erect on the only folding chair Ozzy hadn't used in his construction project, mesmerized by Bob Ross' soothing voice and a magically emerging landscape painting. He sipped water from one of Ozzy's Marvel Universe glasses and said, "I always get thirsty when Bob paints lakes."

"Not a big fan of that kinda art," Ozzy said.

"What artists' work do you admire?

"The old masters—Kirby, Frazetta, Ditko, Wood, Mobius.

"Bob Ross is the master of wet on wet, you know."

"That's a good thing?"

"He is not just an artist; he is a sorcerer. Bob Ross conjures magical landscapes with a two-inch brush."

"Wow, you're waxin' pretty fuckin' poetic today, Ben. Never heard you talk like that."

"I read it somewhere, but it is true. I know what I know."

"You really like this guy."

"I do indeed. He inspires me. I hope to do something truly creative some day."

"Does he ever paint anything besides landscapes?"

"I think not."

"No people—animals?"

"I can't recall seeing him paint anything else, except maybe an occasional seascape."

"If you go into the woods, there are always animals. People too."

"Oh, he often puts a cabin in his paintings, and there are always people inside."

"So, he does paint people?"

"Not exactly. Bob paints his cabins with a light glowing inside, and smoke coming out of the chimney," Ben gestured to the painting on the TV screen, "Like that one. The people are in there. You just can't see them."

"How do you know they aren't out fishing, or off chopping wood or something?"

"Well, Bob says they're in there."

"For fuck's sake, Ben. You're the biggest skeptic of all time, yet you believe there are people in that cabin because Bob Ross says so?"

"It's art, Ozzy. It doesn't have to make sense," Ben said with his nose in the air.

"Okay then, what if the people in the cabin are all dead? You know, like some slasher, in an Easter Bunny suit, is lurking in the woods?" Ozzy pointed to the TV. "He could be hiding right over there, behind that happy fucking tree."

"Now, you're getting the idea, Ozzy."

"And back there, behind those bushes, on the other side of the lake. You can't see 'em, but there's this group of girls from a nearby Bible camp. They're not religious, but sleep-away camp is a good excuse to get away from their fanatical parents."

Ben squints at the painting and nods.

"Wait a minute, they're taking off their clothes," Ozzy said.

Ben teetered on the edge of his seat, "You know what, Ozzy?"

"No, what?"

"If I'm not mistaken, those girls are about to go skinny-dipping."

"Fuck yes they are."

"What do you think of the painting, now?"

"Love it. Bob Ross is a fucking genius."

Ben beamed, "I would love to own a Bob Ross original some day."

"Not me."

"Why not?"

"Too damn intense."

"Perhaps you're right. This one *is* rather provocative."

Ozzy leaned forward. "Oh, shit."

"What?"

"Those girls don't realize Bunny Man is roaming these woods. He's gonna cut 'em to pieces."

"That is terrible."

"Hate to say it, Ben, but I'm afraid he intends to eat them, too."

"How could you possibly know that?"

"Well, you might not have noticed, but there was a pot boiling on the stove, back at the cabin."

"So?"

"There was a human heart in the pot."

Ben reached for the remote. "This painting is too extreme. Perhaps we should change the channel." Ben's eyes widened. "Hold on a minute. Did you see that?"

"What?"

Excitement quickened Ben's reply, "Those boulders Bob just painted in the background."

"What about them?"

"Behind them are several boys from space camp. They are peeping on those girls as they disrobe."

"Yeah, yeah, I see them. I think the girls do too."

"Are the girls waving to the boys to join them?"

"Impossible. Those guys are way too nerdy, and those girls are way too hot."

"No, they are definately waving, and the boys are running over to them."

"Unbelievable."

"Oh my, the boys are taking their clothes off too."

"This painting is really getting good." Ozzy teetered on the edge of his recliner.

Ben looked away, and covered his eyes.

"What's the matter?"

"The athletic girl with the curly, red hair just put the skinny boy's penis in her mouth. He didn't even bother to take off his shoes and socks, or his glasses, for that matter."

"Ya know what that means?"

"They will get married, some day, when they are older. She will win a gold medal at the Olympics, and he will become an astronaut."

Ozzy sprung to his feet and paced around the claustrophobic room. "No, no, no. It means they'll be the first die when Bunny Man tracks them down."

"Why?"

"That's just the rule."

"What kind of rule is that?"

"It's a horror rule. Like vampires can't go out in the sunlight, or silver bullets kill werewolves, or you have to shoot a zombie in the head." Ozzy gestured, penguin skull in hand, like he was giving a TED talk.

"But why do the first teens to have sex have to die first? Why do any of them have to die?"

"Don't know, Ben. I didn't make up the rule."

"Who would make up such a mean-spirited rule?"

"Either John Carpenter or Wes Craven. Not sure which."

"I want those two young people to be happy."

"Sorry. Rules are rules. I gotta pee." Ozzy put down the penguin skull on the arm of his recliner and headed for the bathroom.

He called back to Ben, "Oh, I almost forgot, there's another rule. Keep an eye out for the girl who doesn't have sex. She'll be the only one to make it out of the woods alive."

Ozzy returned from the bathroom to find Ben staring at the television, with terror in his eyes.

Ozzy said, "You okay?"

"I don't want to play this game anymore, Ozzy."

"Hey, I thought we were having fun for a change."

Ben looked directly into Ozzy's eyes, with frightful determination, and said, "It *was* fun—until it wasn't."

Ben bounded in front of the TV to block Ozzy's view of the painting. "For love of Pete, avert your eyes, Ozzy."

Ozzy peered over Ben's bony shoulder and said, "Hey, I want to see the finished painting."

As Bob dabbed in a the final shadows and reflections, Ben's eyes widened. "No, no you do not."

Ozzy backed up a few steps. "Okay, okay. What ever you say."

Ozzy returned to his La-Z-Boy, and went back to work on the mutant skull.

Ben zapped through the channels and stopped on a commercial.

A donut with rainbow sprinkles tumbled through the air in slow motion.

"Ooooh, sprinkles," Ben said.

Ozzy glanced up at the donut as he burrowed a hole in the mutant's skull with the tip of his knife.

"Donut porn used to drive you mad," Ben said as he sipped water from one of Ozzy's Marvel Comics glasses.

"They mean nothing to me now." Ozzy guided a bootlace through the bird's skull, and examined his handiwork.

He blew hard into a hole at the base of the mutant's cranium to dislodge some desiccated bits of brain.

Shriek.

The glass shattered in Ben's hand. "Stop it." Ben said.

Doctor Strange stared up at Ben from a broken shard in his sopping lap.

"That hadda be at least a hundred decibels to break glass like that," Ozzy said.

"Try one-fifty."

"I wonder if those creatures communicate with high frequency sound?" Ozzy said.

"It is certainly possible. There could be ultrasonic, or possibly even infrasonic frequencies we just can't hear."

"Maybe both."

"Did you study bioacoustics at Caltech?"

"Not really. My roommate was doing some cool shit applying echolocation to robotics. He never shut up about it, so I guess I absorbed some of the basics. You get any of that at Harvard?"

"I had a two-hour undergrad seminar. That's it."

"I know one thing. Those fucking freaks have a pack mentality." Ozzy held up the skull. "This guy here, he musta been the alpha freak."

"Perfect, you killed their leader, and now they probably thirst for revenge," Ben said.

Ozzy blew on the skull again.

Shriek.

He grinned and tied the albino penguin skull around his neck.

"Awesome."

Run Roland Run

"Yeah, yeah, I know, I know. You're probably right, but it's not my damn fault, man. It's just too fucking easy," said Roland Bouchard.

The cockpit of the DeHavilland, Twin Otter airplane seemed more cramped than usual as, Chuck, his best friend and eco-tourism partner, read Roland the riot act. The lanky, gray haired pilot shook his head in disapproval as he stared out the windshield at the sterile Antarctic icescape that stretched beyond the horizon.

Chuck said, "Damn it, Roland, your penile polar adventures are going to bite us in the ass one of these days."

"They always start it, man," Roland said.

"And why do you suppose that is?" Chuck raised a brow and smirked, "You are not a handsome man."

"I do have mad charisma, though." Roland rubbed his forearm on the shoulder of Chuck's vintage bomber jacket as if some of his charm would rub off.

Chuck said, "With two ex-wives and three kids in college, I'd rather have cash than charisma."

Roland grinned, "Some guys got it, some guys–"

"Are only charismatic south of the 70th parallel?"

"Fuck you."

"You're pushing forty and you haven't had a single long-term relationship."

Roland said, "You should see the way the women look at me, back in Montreal. They always look so pissed off."

Chuck stifled a laugh.

"Not funny, my man. It's because I'm black, ya know."

"They look at all the guys like that."

"Our touristes femmes never look at me like that. They look at me with hungry eyes. Hungry fucking eyes. Know what I mean?"

"The Asian ones, Right?"

"Well, yeah. So what?"

"It's because they've never seen a black dude before. They want to find out if what they say about that certain part of the male anatomy is true."

"That's racist, mythological shit."

Chuck laughed, "Just because *you* don't have a big—"

"Hey, hey, hey, man, when we did the Polar Plunge at Port Charcot, the water was muthafuckin' freezing—all right."

"Yeah, yeah, yeah. Just do me a favor, put a muzzle on that thing and keep it away from the customers. It's un-fucking-professional."

"Okay, okay, but I'm not making any promises."

"I'm serious. You're going to ruin our reputation."

"What happens in Antarctica stays in Antarctica, baby."

Chuck groaned and said, "Get on the horn and give Pratt and Eaton a heads-up. We'll be there at 0900."

Roland saluted and said, "Roger that, captain cockblocker."

Roland toggled the radio on and adjusted the volume in his headset, "Yo, Earthwatch One, this is Otter 1029F, pick up your socks and underwear, we'll be there in 90. Over."

Static.

"Come in Earthwatch One. Do you read me, over?"

Static.

Roland handed the headset to Chuck, "Looks like nobody's home."

Chuck checked the frequency, "Don't sweat it, they know we're coming."

The plane lurched starboard.

Frenetic chatter from the cabin drowned out the drone of the twin turboprop Pratt & Whitney engines.

Chuck turned to Roland, "Better see what's up with the passengers."

Roland adjusted his tie, unbuckled his seatbelt, and steadied himself in the cockpit doorway.

All twenty eco-tourists crowded the starboard side of the cabin. They snapped pictures out the plane's panoramic windows like possessed paparazzi, chattering in their native tongues.

Roland crooned into the PA microphone, "For your own safety, please return to your—" The mic was dead. He dropped it and grabbed the amplified megaphone he used on the tours, "Yo, listen up people. Return to your damn seats."

The preoccupied tourists ignored his command.

Roland elbowed his way down the crowded aisle, pushed a telephoto lens aside, and looked out a window. "Holy shit."

On the ice below, a vast colony of penguins waddled as one.

Roland stumbled back to the cockpit, "Check out your three o'clock, man."

Chuck glanced out the side window, and did a double take, "What the fuck?"

Roland said, "Ever seen so many penguins this far inland?"

Chuck shook his head, "I've never seen this many penguins anywhere."

Roland winked, "Let's put this baby down and give the day-trippers the thrill of a lifetime."

Chuck said, "What about our Earthwatch One tour?"

"They can wait. We'll only lose an hour tops."

Chuck grinned, "Yeah, what the hell. Why not?"

~

The ski equipped Twin Otter plowed the thin layer of snow that blanketed the mile-thick ice sheet, and skidded to a stop.

Roland and the tour group hustled down the plane's retractable stairs.

The tourists fanned out on the ice.

In the distance, the undulating black and white mass approached. Fast.

The camera and cell phone brandishing sightseers jabbered excitedly.

Roland struck a pose on the plane's ski strut. He whispered into his megaphone, but it was still absurdly loud, "Yo, people, quiet down now. You'll scare the damn penguins."

Chuck surveyed the scene from the top of the passenger stairs.

The penguins converged on the lively group.

Roland said, "Listen up, people. These penguins seem unusually friendly, but please do not feed them. You might make them sick."

The penguins were now only a few feet away from Roland, "These penguins appear to be Eudyptes Crestata, commonly known as Rock Hoppers because they like to hop."

A mutant penguin leaped at the nearest tourist and impaled him in the belly."

A portly Russian man dropped to his knees.

Scarlet goose feathers burst from the gory hole in Dmitri Titov's designer parka.

The mutant burrowed into his abdomen.

Roland watched in disbelief as the creature's flippers disappeared into the bloody hole.

Roland staggered backward and dropped his megaphone. He stumbled up the stairs, paused at the open door, and looked down at Dmitri, a good-natured oligarch and avid collector of porcelain penguinalia. Roland enjoyed making Dimitri laugh. The guy loved to laugh, but he wasn't laughing now.

Dmitri's screams gave way to the sickening sound of cracking ribs.

Roland wanted to help, but all he could do was watch.

Dmitri's mouth opened wide. Too wide.

Roland hoped he wouldn't call for help because there was there was nothing he could do.

The mutant's head burst out of Dmitri's gaping mouth. His dislocated jaw became a hideous garland of bloody, bubbling saliva and broken teeth.

The creature's wild, red eyes scanned the tourists. Beyond pure blood lust, Roland sensed a ruthless intelligence, common to all predators.

The creature wriggled and thrashed in an effort to exit the tourist's distorted maw, but only managed to wriggle out half way. Dmitri's corpse flopped around on the ice beside Roland's abandoned megaphone like fresh-caught fish on the deck of a trawler.

The monstrous fowl screeched, amplified by Roland's megaphone.

The ravenous horde screeched a deafening reply.

Roland covered his ears, lost his grip on the railing, and tumbled down the stairs.

Chuck appeared in the doorway, brandishing a flare gun. He reached down to hoist Roland back up, as the creatures attacked, en-masse.

Chuck said, "C'mon, c'mon, get your ass up here."

Roland reached up to Chuck. He only made it to the second step. The snapping, snipping, slashing mutants shredded Roland's right thigh and groin. As he tumbled backward, Roland's agonizing wail joined the chorus of screaming tourists. He hit the ice hard, but the pain from the bites made the impact a welcome diversion. Roland kept his eyes on Chuck, at the top of the air-stairs, as he rolled toward the slaughter.

Chuck leveled his flare gun at the attackers and fired. The flare parted the charging horde.

Roland could barely make out the silhouettes of his group through the swath of red smoke and flaming mutants.

Chuck reloaded and fired again and again until the creatures retreated a few yards from the plane.

Roland crawled across the crimson ice to the plane's front ski strut and propped himself up. His blood-soaked hand shook as he fumbled in his coat pocket. He pulled out a pack of Du Mauriers and lit one up. He took a long, slow drag and watched the best part of his charisma disappear down a voracious monstrosity's gullet.

Roland was more concerned with the fate of his tour group than his own questionable future. He tried to stand up, but the severity of his injuries made that impossible. Roland wasn't a student of human anatomy, but he knew that something vital to standing had been severed. The electrical jolts of pain in his groin surged to every extremity, and fried the circuits in his brain. The searing current tripped a breaker in his head and the pain subsided to a pulsing throb.

A laundry list of what-ifs raced through his mind. What if they never landed and continued on to Earthwatch One as planned, was at the top of the list.

Guilt, frustration, and terror overpowered Roland's sense of reason, but it didn't matter because there was nothing rational about the situation.

Things like this don't happen. Penguins don't just turn into monsters. I can't die yet. I have library books to return. Laundry to pick up. That cat that comes around to feed. This can't be real.

But the terrified tourists' screams were all too real.

The tourists scattered, but there was no place to go.

The mutant penguins had cut them off from the plane.

Roland watched the tourists fall one by one into a screeching meat grinder of razor beaks and slashing talons.

Roland tried, but couldn't take his eyes off the carnage. His customers' names and faces flashed through his mind, only to vanish in the swirling blood-spatter mist that rose and evaporated in the frigid polar breeze.

A pack of mutants savagely pecked a shrieking woman's skull. Roland was fairly certain it was Dandan Hon, but hoped he was wrong. He hated to admit it, but he liked the way he couldn't understand a word she said when they made love in almost every science station bathroom on the frozen continent. Though he didn't speak a word of Cantonese, he knew her impassioned declarations were plenty dirty. Urgent words spoken in low guttural tones needed no translation.

Roland realized he never heard a woman scream except in the movies. It killed him to hear Dandan scream now.

When the hideous mutations cracked her skull open, the screaming stopped. They gorged on the rich, gray brain pudding inside.

Before they had pecked her cranium clean, first one, then all the little monsters disgorged their gory meal. They continued to heave until steaming suet littered the surrounding ice. The sickening smorgasbord of carnage attracted another swarm of scavenging monstrosities. They devoured the loathsome left-overs, and heaved that up too, attracting even more of the vile creatures.

This was no YouTube video. This was real, and this was now.

Not knowing whether he was going to bleed out before he froze to death in the loneliest place on Earth, was too much for Roland to process.

He began to laugh until he couldn't catch his breath. Then he wept. The tears stung as they froze on his cheeks. At least the cold burn of despair was proof of life—what little of it was left.

The insatiable little monsters broke ranks and began fighting among themselves for unrecognizable scraps of raw meat.

Chuck waved to his mangled passengers.

Roland yelled, "Go, go, go, get in the plane!"

The few sightseers who still had legs struggled up the stairs dragging their attackers with them.

Chuck pulled mangled day-trippers into the plane, and slammed the door, but not before several mutants bounded aboard.

On the ice, the hellish screaming and screeching gave way to the roar of the Twin Otter's engines.

Steam rose from the widening puddle of Roland's blood that pooled around the plane's ski strut.

The glowing stub of his cigarette tumbled from Roland's lips and sputtered out in the scarlet puddle.

The Twin Otter lurched forward. Roland rolled off the strut, and onto the ice.

The brutish cold dulled the pain enough for Roland to prop himself up on his elbows. He watched the plane's skis shimmy as it pulled away, leaving a single red stripe on the ancient ice.

Roland squinted from the sunlight that glittered on the endless white wilderness like a million diamonds.

He glimpsed the logo on the plane's fuselage as it gained speed. *ROLANDS POLAR ADVENTURES.*

How could he not have noticed? All these years and he never noticed the graphic designer and the sign painter left off the apostrophe in Roland's.

Too late to fix it now. How come no one ever pointed it out? Someone hadda fucking notice. What about Chuck, our website designer, or some retired English professor on the tour? Were they all afraid to hurt my feelings? Did they think I was stupid? That I didn't know the difference. They're the stupid ones—stupid fucks, stupid, stupid, stupid.

Roland watched the plane take off.

His pain took off with it. Only the cold remained.

His vision dimmed, but he couldn't keep his eyes off the Twin Otter.

It rose like a lonesome spirit in the cloudless sky, then it wobbled, and plunged downward in an ever-tightening spiral.

Roland didn't hear the Twin Otter crash, but he saw the fireball. He marveled at the way the smoke sketched awkward shapes in the empty sky, like a self-conscious art student's first charcoal drawing.

The missing apostrophe didn't matter now. Nothing mattered now. A perverse sense of relief swept over him as his cone of vision narrowed to a single speck of light.

Damn, it's cold down here. Gettin' dark too.

Roland wondered if death would be colder than the cold and darker than the dark that surrounded him. He never thought much about death. Why should he?

Hey, it's always the other guy who dies in a car crash, or from some horrible cancer, or being crushed under hoarder-high stacks of old newspapers. Millions of people die every damn year in wars and natural disasters—but not me. Ha—guess it's my turn to be someone else's other guy.

Roland was invincible—until now, when his own, private, personal death was eminent. He was unsure of so many things. No time left to figure anything out. Why even try?

At least Roland was certain of one thing, what happens in Antarctica stays in Antarctica—for-fucking-ever.

Tanya and Teller

Ozzy checked his watch, and aimed the remote at the television like a phaser set to kill. He zapped through the channels like they were Romulans. When he eased his thumb off the rubbery arrow, there was Tanya Brown. He stopped, grinned, and let the remote drop to the floor.

Ozzy's new favorite show was *Cardio Kickboxing with Tanya*. He spent an hour, every day, with the big, blonde, body builder as she worked out on the beach with her petite Hawaiian assistant, Kulani.

Ben thrashed on his cot and pulled his blanket over his head. "Could you please turn that infernal television *off*?"

"No."

"Then I will."

"No way. Gotta date with my baby."

Tanya's shorts rode up as she stretched.

"Whoa, baby," Ozzy said, "buns of fucking steel."

Ben peeked out from the covers.

Ozzy joined in the, aerobic kickboxing exercises.

"I'm impressed. You can actually keep up with her now," Ben said.

"It's easy with my Tanya."

"You must have lost a hundred pounds in the last few months."

Ozzy executed a complex series of punches and kicks, sweeping high, then low, without so much as a huff or a puff.

Sweat glistened on Tanya's powerful thighs.

Ozzy glanced over at Ben and did a double take.

Ben ogled the TV with an uncharacteristic grin. But what

commanded Ozzy's attention was further south. Ben's blanket displayed the unmistakable architecture of a boner tent.

"Hey, hey, hey, that's my girl, you pervert," said Ozzy.

Nobody looks at my Tanya like that.

"I repaired the television. I'll watch anything I please."

Ozzy stopped pummeling the defenseless air that swirled between the cold floor and the low ceiling.

"She'd never fall for a skinny ass weasel like you."

"If you must know, I was looking at Kulani."

Ozzy blocked Ben's view of the TV. "Yeah right."

"You wouldn't stand a chance with a woman like Tanya Brown," Ben said, "Besides, they're lesbians."

"I'm so sure."

Kulani steadied Tanya's hips as she squatted with free-weights.

"Look, they can't keep their hands off one another," Ben said.

"She's spotting her. It's a safety thing."

"It's a lesbian thing."

"Ain't so, Pinocchio." Ben pushed down on the bulge under his blanket, but it immediately pupped the tent up again.

"Frankly, I'm shocked you'd make such a sexist, homophobic remark," Ozzy said.

"I, I, I—"

"I'm well aware that if I met Tanya back in the world she'd shun me for the overweight geek I am. She's a fantasy, just like your precious Lorelei."

"Leave her out of it."

"Have you even been with a real woman?"

"None of your business."

"Internet girls, that's your speed, right?"

"I'll have you know, I had unprotected sex with Yolanda Styles at the Alternative Health Expo."

Ben proudly pulled his lower lip down and flaunted a lesion. "I even contracted a venereal disease, a nasty case of oral herpes."

Ozzy roared.

Ben stormed into the bathroom and locked the door.

Ozzy watched TV by himself. "Oh Ben, the news is on. Are you sure you want to leave me alone with Lorelei?"

The bathroom door creaked open. Ben traipsed out.

On TV, Lorelei Teller, an imposing newswoman in her late 30s, read the news. "Prince Paddy Roy Bates of Sealand announced today the world's smallest nation will soon be the site of a secure internet server farm and global networking hub."

Ben gazed at Lorelei with a look of avarice.

On screen, a huge steel platform with a rusty superstructure rested atop two massive concrete pylons towering one hundred feet above a raging sea. "The Principality of Sealand, an abandoned World War II anti-aircraft fort, is located in the North Sea, six miles off the southeast coast of England."

"If they put a lab on that thing, they could do all kinds of cool shit. Stem cell research, cloning—without government interference," Ozzy said.

Lorelei's face filled the screen. "In 1968, Sealand's independence was upheld in the British courts because it stands in international waters."

Ben Eaton whimpered, holding his head, but he couldn't seem to keep it on straight.

"With all the totally amazing women on television, why her?" Ozzy said.

"Those lips. Just look at those lips."

"Yeah, so?"

"Are you blind? See how full and pouty they are."

"Collagen."

Lorelei continued, "The British government fears Sealand will become a safe haven for tax shelters, internet pornography and IP piracy."

"Did you see that? Ooooooh," Eaton said, with Basset Hound eyes.

"What?"

"There—right there." The corner of Lorelei's mouth turned up ever so slightly, a cross between a cynical sneer and a faint smile.

"I'm simply mad about the little thing she does with her mouth," Eaton said.

"It's some kinda neurological condition."

She creeps me out, for real.

"She smiles like that because she knows things."

Oh brother.

"She knows what they give her to read."

Eaton shook and gestured wildly. "She knows far more than she's telling about me and the way I feel about her."

"You're definitely one news break over the line." Ozzy helped Eaton to his cot and pulled a blanket over him. "That's enough TV for tonight, little man."

Dire Disclosure

Down in the Pit, Eaton mindlessly mopped the floor, circling the spot where Ozzy exercised.

That's weird. He's never done that before.

Steam rose from the cold concrete causing the Pit to reek like a human kennel.

He's gone and disturbed the grime patina that sealed the stink in all this time.

Ozzy did sit-ups as he watched one of those world's funniest video shows.

A skateboarder sailed over an outdoor stair railing, onto the sidewalk and—*smack*—right into a parking meter.

"Yowwwch," Ozzy said, "Why is that funny?"

"Human suffering is never amusing, Ozzy."

Next, a hunter snuck up on a moose in a clearing. The huge buck charged, planted its antlers in the hunter's ass and flipped him into a tree.

Eaton cackled.

"What's so funny, Ben?" Ozzy said.

"Do I need to explain comedic irony?"

"Let's just eat breakfast."

Eaton stopped laughing, "We ate the last of the tofu yesterday."

"Is that an example of comedic irony?"

"No, Ozzy, that is a fact."

"Get outta here."

"The tofu is all gone—finito."

Ozzy checked the boxes for himself—empty. "What the hell are we gonna do now?"

"I suppose we could go on a fast."

"When there's a taco truck around the corner, it's fasting. When you're marooned in Ant-fucking-arctica, I believe it's called starving to death."

"Have you ever gone on a damn fast?"

"No, but I bet you've been on more fasts than Mahatma Gandhi.

"I've gone on a number of fasts. One time I fasted for two weeks. It was incredibly purifying."

Ozzy grabbed the remote. He pushed the buttons hard and fast.

"Give me that thing." Eaton pried the remote from Ozzy's hand.

Zap, an old cartoon of a cat chasing a mouse with a hatchet flashed on the TV screen.

After Weeks of Fasting

Ozzy paced in front of the television, shaking and sweating. The walls of the Pit expanded and contracted in Ozzy's peripheral vision. He tried to focus on the TV monitor, the only stationary point in the undulating room. Hewell Howser chatted with a Mexican chef as he tossed jiggling tripe and a calf's foot into a huge, steaming pot.

Hewell said, "Now, I've heard there's nothing as good as good menudo, and nothing as bad as bad menudo."

The chef held up a big brush. "You have to clean the tripe really good."

Ozzy sat on his cot with his head between his knees. "I feel sick."

"The menudo is making me nauseous too," Eaton said.

"It's not the menudo. It's this fucking fasting."

"You're a walking biohazard. Pesticides, pollution, preservatives, they collect in your fat. The fast is just flushing them out."

Ozzy rubbed his face. The nerve endings in his forehead and cheeks tingled with scurrying spiders and foraging ants.

"Drink more water and lie down," Eaton said, "You'll feel much better in a day or two."

"If I don't die first."

"What doesn't kill us makes us—"

"*Wish* we were dead?"

As the days dawdled by, Eaton gave his friend sips of water. Ozzy was grateful, and tried to smile when Ben offered hollow words of encouragement, but flexing his facial muscles was far too strenuous. When Ben fed him gummy Star Wars vitamins,

Ozzy didn't have the strength to chew, so Vader and Boba Fett just melted away in his half-open mouth for hours.

Ozzy gazed up at Ben who loomed over him like a blurry specter of death. The bony apparition extended his hands with an offering.

Should I take it? It seems important. Maybe it's a key that opens a portal to another dimension and I can get out of here.

Ozzy reached out with what little strength he had left to accept the mysterious offering. Ben put the TV remote in Ozzy's hand, but Ozzy was too weak to push the buttons. He drifted in and out of consciousness as an endless stream of TV shows played on in their little hole in the ice at the bottom of the world. The shows' characters and storylines often hijacked Ozzy's dreamy delirium. In one Lynchian mashup, Ozzy joined forces with Jerry Seinfeld and Doctor Who to battle vampires with Buffy in Downton Abbey.

Rapid Rejuvenation and Dismal Degeneration

Ozzy's eyes fluttered open. He eased out of his La-Z-Boy. On TV, Tanya and Kulani kick boxed, on the beach, to Deep Forest's Franco-Pygmy, techno beat.

"How long have I been fucked up?"

"Almost three weeks. How do you feel?"

"Great, actually. Kinda buzzy all over."

Eaton collapsed on his cot, wheezing.

Shit, Ben's got that Faces of Death look.

Ozzy brought Eaton some water, but his hands shook so hard, he could barely hold the cup.

Ozzy kick boxed with Tanya. "If I don't burn up some of this bizarro energy, I'll explode."

He worked out hard, singing along with the Pygmies. "Dit, dit, dit de da de…"

Ozzy breezed through a grueling burpee set, mirroring Tanya's every move. He dropped to the floor, did a push-up, jumped into a squat and rocketed to his feet. Ozzy billowed white puffs like a steam-powered automaton, adding some welcome humidity to the cold, dry air. Sweat soaked his Gortex snowsuit. The Pit smelled like high school locker room, and he liked it. The familiar burn returned. His heart pumped life back into every muscle in his body and jumpstarted his sluggish brain.

"Give it a rest," Eaton said, "you're making me dizzy."

"This whole fasting thing is amazing."

"Glad you feel well. I feel dreadful."

"You're just going through what I went through."

"I'm afraid not, Ozzy. You're burning fat. I'm burning muscle and organ tissue."

"What, like your dick?

"No, like my heart, and my liver, and my kidneys, and my lungs."

Ozzy reclined in his La-Z-Boy.

Eaton slept on his cot.

Eaton's girlfriend read the news.

"Hey Ben, Lorelei's here to see you," Ozzy said.

Eaton tried to smooth his matted hair and struggled to sit up, "Quick, change the channel. I don't want Lorelei to see me like this."

The covers fell away. Eaton wore only droopy, shit-stained jockey shorts and snow boots as he shuffled to the bathroom.

Ozzy laughed as he watched an old *Ren and Stimpy* cartoon.

He heard sobbing and looked into the darkened bathroom.

Eaton slouched on the toilet with his arms folded around his chest, like he was trying to hold himself together. Then Ozzy started sobbing too.

Frightful Food

Ozzy struggled to cinch his parka hood with heavy gloves on.

Eaton languished on his cot.

Ozzy squatted next to him. "C'mon, Ben, get up."

Eaton strained to sit up. "What?"

Ozzy helped Eaton to his feet, guided him to the door and pointed at the bolt. "When I close the door, lock it. When I get back, let me in—*fast*."

"Where are you going?"

"Thought I'd pick up some take-out. I bet those mutants taste just like chicken."

Ozzy opened the door. Wind blew trash around the room. An acrid odor hung in the frigid air. He stepped into the darkness. The heavy door slammed shut.

Ozzy waited for the bolt to snap closed and stepped forward.

A sickening *crunch* reverberated in the pitch-black stairwell.

"What the—" Ozzy turned on his flashlight. "—fuck."

A face stared up at him with hollow eye sockets. Desiccated flesh clung to the skull. Its rib cage protruded from a shredded white parka with a red wolf patch. The remaining bits and pieces were unidentifiable.

Ozzy sidestepped the corpse and bounded up the stairs.

On the ice, Ozzy's flashlight cast grotesque shadows in the twisted wreckage of the devastated compound. He pulled a claw hammer out of his parka, held it high and shined his light in a drum—empty. He swept the ruins with his flashlight—nothing.

Ozzy approached a gutted shed. Tools littered the ice. Ozzy

found a geologist's pick and dropped his hammer. Further on, he dropped the geologist's pick in favor of a formidable ice ax. He felt its weight, grinned.

Ozzy spotted a lone mutant sniffing a steaming mound of monster scat beside some scattered bones and a toppled anemometer.

Don't do it. Just waddle away. Don't you eat that shit right before we eat you.

The creature pecked the mound and plucked out a stringy morsel.

Ozzy inched toward the beast.

You're a big boy. Dinner for two.

The mutant tossed his head back and gulped down the vile tidbit.

Ozzy lunged, swung his ice ax and hit the creature in the middle of its back with enough force to send the mutant tumbling several yards. He jogged after it into an open space. The creature lay motionless face down on the ice. Ozzy hoisted it by its feet and examined it closely.

You are one ugly, ugly motherfucker. Never eaten genetically modified meat before. Just hope you're not too radioactive.

Ozzy headed back to the Pit, dragging the mutant by its feet.

Screech.

The creature squirmed out of Ozzy grip and leaped out of reach.

Ozzy took off after him on the open ice, but slid to a stop. Thousands of red eyes flickered beyond the debris field.

Holy shit.

He turned to run, but pivoted to face the advancing horde.

Fuck it. I'm not leaving here empty handed.

He charged, brandishing his ice ax, and let out a battle cry. The vicious mutations just keep coming.

Ozzy reconsidered his plan of attack and slid to a stop.

This is nuts.

He retreated, tripping over debris on the slippery ice as he hauled ass for the stairwell.

The creatures converged as Ozzy stumbled down the icy stairs.

He threw his ice ax at them. They attacked it with such ferocity he peed himself a little bit.

Bang—bang—bang.

Ozzy pounded on the bolted door.

"Open up, Ben."

No reply.

C'mon, C'mon.

Bang—bang—bang.

Ozzy pounded harder and so did his heart. He scanned the top of the stairs for mutants.

For fuck's sake, Ben. Open the damn door.

The bolt rattled on the other side of the door.

A fumbling rattle sounded from the bolt on the other side of the door.

Red eyes glowed at the top of the stairs.

Ozzy kicked the door and shouted, "Lemme in!"

More fumbling, then the bolt snapped open.

Ozzy rammed the door with his shoulder.

It only opened a few inches.

"Out of the way, damn it."

Ozzy pushed against the door with his full weight.

The door burst open.

He bounded in, hurling Eaton aside.

Ozzy kicked the door shut, and slammed the bolt closed.

Ben lay sprawled out on the floor.

Ozzy rushed to his side, carried him to his cot and set him down.

Eaton went through the motions of opening a lock. "I tried, but I just couldn't seem to open the—"

"You did good, Ben. You opened the door real good."

Weary Wishes

Later that night, the only light in the Pit came from a muscle car auction on the television. Ozzy didn't care about the gleaming examples of American automotive might, but he did care about his partner. Ozzy watched his friend watch the show. Eaton's sunken eyes were wet with longing, yet they still sparkled with wonder as the cars rolled by, each one more magnificent and valuable than the last.

Eaton pulled out clumps of hair as the auctioneer hypnotized the wealthy bidders with his melodic patter.

How much longer can he go on like this? How much longer can I?

A steak house commercial came on. As country music played, a knife sliced through a two-inch thick charbroiled steak. Bloody juice gushed from the steaming slit.

"That doesn't look so bad," Eaton said.

Ozzy laughed. "That's funny, it was actually grossing me out."

Eaton rocked as he talked, "I never had a convertible. I want to own a metallic, blue GTO, a classic, with black upholstery."

"You will."

"I want to drive it with the top down on a desert highway at night."

"You will."

"I want to get a tattoo, an eyeball with wings, or maybe the name of some girl I meet in a bar."

"You will. You will."

"I haven't eaten meat in eight years, Ozzy."

"When we get outta here, I'll take you to one of those steak houses. We'll eat T-bones till we shit hamburgers."

The television flickered like an electronic campfire. It bathed the cluttered, tomb-sized room in a ghastly artificial glow. Grotesque shadows slithered across the cold, bleak walls.

Right before Ozzy dozed off, a man with a gray ponytail wearing a Hawaiian shirt was the high bidder on a 1969 Dodge Charger Daytona.

Eaton Excitations

Eaton squirmed on his cot.

Eaton moaned as he clutched his distended abdomen. He shot up like a steel spring had snapped in his back.

He leaped to the floor and crouched on his haunches like an animal.

His eyes burned wild, darting back and forth until they fixed on a roll of thick nylon cord.

He lurched across the room.

Eaton's bony fingers seized the cord.

He clinched the rope in his teeth, and crawled on his hands and knees to the cot where Ozzy slept.

Eaton lashed the cord securely to a leg of Ozzy's sturdy cot, slid it underneath, and wrapped it around Ozzy's chest.

He made the binding snug, but not tight enough to disturb his sleeping partner.

He repeated the maneuver until he had worked his way down to Ozzy's ankles.

Eaton tied the ends to the foot of the cot, and scooted back to admire his work.

Ozzy lay helpless, wrapped up like a mummy.

An inhuman euphoria consumed Ben. He tried to contain his delight, but could not. A maniacal chuckle rumbled deep inside his sunken chest. He clinched his jaw tight and tried to hold it in, but that only made it more hideous when it wheezed through the gaps in his sinister grin.

Eaton hopped around the room, beating the cold concrete floor with his fists.

An endless stream of auction patter, from the television, masked the dull thuds, and insane chuckling.

Eaton scanned the room and found what he was looking for. Above the door, on the top shelf of the industrial Metro shelving, the object of his unwholesome attention waited patiently for use—the medical kit.

He wrestled the box to the floor, fumbled with the clasp, and popped the lid. There were enough medical supplies inside to perform a minor operation—and Eaton knew how to use them all.

He rifled through the kit until he found a scalpel and a butterfly bandage. He snatched them up, scooted to the foot of Ozzy's cot.

Eaton lifted the heavy blanket and exposed Ozzy's feet.

He removed a thick wool sock from his partner's sweaty, right foot.

It looked so plump, so pink, and so, so naked.

The ecstatic Eaton spun in circles and growled. His hands shook with anticipation as he ripped off the plastic cover of the scalpel with his teeth.

A kaleidoscope of flashing colors from the television shimmered on its keen cutting edge.

Eaton held Ozzy's big toe steady and plunged the scalpel into its meaty underside.

He sliced deep, and thrust downward with one sure stroke. The moist, callused skin was no match for the surgical steel. It split open like a round, ripe fig.

Tortured Toe

Ozzy's eyes sprang open. "Owshit! What the fuck?"

The incision was deep and clean. Blood gushed from the gaping wound.

Eaton dropped the scalpel and positioned his head under the warm, red spring that flowed from the obscene gash.

Ozzy raised his head enough to see Eaton close his eyes, and opened his mouth wide.

A wave of nausea crashed over Ozzy as the sweet, salty serum splash into Eaton's mouth, and splatter over his cheeks and chin.

Ozzy thrashed, but the rope didn't budge.

Eaton dropped to his knees and approached the gory gusher from above—so as not to waste a single drop of the life sustaining liquid.

Ozzy stiffened in horror as his demented partner popped the entire toe in his mouth, and pursed his cracked lips tight around the plump, hairy shaft. Eaton sucked with a strong even suction. Ozzy's blood gushed over his tongue and spilled down his gurgling gullet. The vegetarian-turned-vampire moaned with disgusting delight.

Ozzy pressed his chin to his chest and watched Eaton nurse his big toe like a hideous bony baby.

"What the fuck!" Ozzy struggled, "What the fucking fuck, Ben. For fucksake, stop it!"

Eaton's eyes fluttered open, then drooped in loathsome contentment. The rhythm of the slurping lulled him into a sleepy state of ecstasy. His eyes rolled back as he moaned with sickening satisfaction.

"Oh shit!" Ozzy closed his eyes in terror and disgust.

Eaton's head shot upright with a quick reptilian jerk. A menacing grin spread across his gaunt face. He bared his blood-streaked teeth and giggled fiendishly. Coagulated blood bubbled between his crooked incisors and spilled over his cracked lips.

Ozzy pleaded and strained against his bonds, "Untie me, Ben. Now! Untie me and we'll forget this ever happened. We gotta a lotta shows to see. We can watch anything *you* want."

Eaton wiggled Ozzy's big toe. "This little piggy—"

"Yeah, yeah, he went to the fucking market," Ozzy said, "Just untie me, all right."

Eaton ducked under the cot and tittered playfully.

Ozzy strained to see Eaton. "Where are you, damn it? This isn't—"

"Funny?" Eaton said as he popped up like a hellish, jaundiced, Jack-in-the-box.

Ozzy jolted. "Shit, Ben, untie me. I gotta pee." He grimaced as he tried to hold his water.

Eaton flicked his tongue over the bleeding gash—mocking the way Ozzy had teased him with his chocolate cupcake.

Ozzy pleaded, "C'mon, I really gotta piss."

Eaton quivered with anticipation as he stared at Ozzy's toe. The nauseating slurping and brutish suction began again.

Despair overwhelmed Ozzy as his bladder control wavered. He let it all go. Urine flooded his snow pants, seeped through the canvas cot and dribbled onto the floor. Steam rose from the yellow puddle on the cold concrete.

Eaton's eyes rolled back as he sucked. Ozzy looked away in revulsion.

After a few minutes, Eaton wiped his chin. "That's enough—*for now.*"

Ozzy strained against his bonds as Eaton squeezed the gushing incision closed, licked it clean, and cinched it tight with a butterfly bandage.

The blood-fiend slithered under Ozzy's cot.

Ozzy stared up at the ceiling, as Eaton panted and wheezed

below him. Glowing patches of lichen created random silhouettes that found form in Ozzy's suffocating terror. All manner of ghastly apparitions took form in his ominous imaginings. Skull faces with mocking eyes merged with luminous renderings of lewd gargoyles, and grotesque chimaeras. Staring up at the phosphorescent fresco only intensified Ozzy's dread, but eventually, he nodded off from emotional exhaustion.

Ozzy awoke to the giddy sound of a little girl giggling. For a moment, he thought he was back in the world—but it was Eaton, crouched at the foot of his cot.

The madman peeled back the bandage and pinched the wound on the swollen toe. It popped open like a soft plastic coin purse.

Eaton's eyes widened as blood gushed from the clean, deep slit. He quivered in anticipation, then started nursing.

Ozzy shuddered and clinched his fists. When the ordeal was over, Eaton returned to their usual TV routine until it was time for dinner. More nursing, then more TV. The sickening cycle went on for days. Ozzy became numb to the horror and accepted it with grim repulsion.

After a while, Eaton actually looked a little better. There was a hint of color in his sunken cheeks, but his mental faculties continued to deteriorate. It was impossible for Ozzy to talk to him anymore. Any communication between them was totally one-sided. Eaton had become a monstrous, inhuman fiend.

Friend or Fiend

Two days passed.

Ozzy craned his neck to keep an eye on Eaton as he circled the cot, shaking his head and muttering to himself. "No, no, no, no. I know what I know."

Ozzy could barely recognize his friend. Ben had always been skinny, but now he looked more like one of those screaming, Peruvian mummies, as he pulled at the slack flesh on his gaunt cheeks. His yellow conjunctiva, framed by anemic, pink inner eyelids, made Ozzy look away.

The wild man approached his captive's bandaged toe, touched the soiled dressing with his cadaverous index finger, and leaped back. He licked his lips and approached again, but instead of peeling back the bandage, he pounced on Ozzy's chest, and leered down at him. "You think you are *sooo* smart. Mister big man, with your big plans. I am smart too. I know what I know, what I know, what I know."

Ozzy turned his head to avoid the foul shower of rancid spit that spattered with each delirious word.

Ozzy strained against his bonds, more out of habit than any real hope of breaking free. He gasped for breath. The nylon cord that restrained him was tight, but the weight of his deranged captor, crouching on his chest, was the primary cause of his worsening asphyxia.

Ozzy wasn't afraid any more. All that remained of his shattered psyche was a pernicious sadness that squirmed into his bones and wormed its way deep into his icy marrow.

Eaton squealed like a child on pony ride with each heave

Ozzy's chest. He gestured wildly, "Can't fool me! You have a plan—" He wagged his bony finger in Ozzy's face. "—a venomous plan."

"No plans here, Ben. I'm *wide* open."

"You're trying to kill me," Eaton said, "Your blood is poison." He pulled at his flesh, "Look at me."

"C'mon."

"You're a snake, stalking your prey. I know what I know."

"No way."

"I'll show you."

If I'm going to die, it's going to be in a happy place.

Ozzy clinched his eyes shut and found himself standing in the hallway of Jonas E. Salk Middle School. Chattering voices, clanging lockers, and trudging feet reverberated in the cavernous corridor.

February 14th held no significance to Ozzy's eighth-grade self—until Emily tapped him on the shoulder. She was usually quite pale, which contrasted nicely with her raven hair. But today, her face was bright red as she handed him a big, black envelope and smiled.

That's weird, Emily hasn't smiled since she started dressing like Lydia from Beetlejuice, in the seventh grade.

Before he had a chance to replace his shocked expression with one of gratitude, she disappeared into the hustling herd of tweens, without saying a word.

Ozzy examined the ominous envelope from every angle. He held it up to the fluorescent light to see if anything was written on it.

Nothing.

The hallway fell silent. The third period bell rang. He stuffed the envelope in his backpack and sprinted down the empty hallway.

He was tardy for his American history class, but it didn't matter—not when there was a mystery to solve.

He fished the envelope from is backpack and hid it inside his open history book.

Andrew Jackson will have to win the battle of New Orleans without me, today.

Ozzy faked a cough and ripped the envelope open with his pencil. Sweat beaded his forehead, and his pulse quickened as he slid a hand painted card from the worrisome envelope.

Had Emily painted this herself? Of course she had—but why?

The artwork was expressive and messy, yet totally realistic. Crows pecked at a bloody, anatomically correct human heart. A border of tiny skulls framed the gruesome tableau.

He gasped as he read the spooky, hand-drawn type: *My heart bleeds for you.*

Shit.

He wasn't positive, but he was pretty sure this was a Valentine's Day card. He'd seen plenty before in the drug store, and affixed to the refrigerator door, at home, with a magnet, but never anything like this.

What if this isn't a Valentine at all? It could be a threat or some kind of curse.

Emily was rather witchy, and he did torment her, on a daily basis, before she turned to the dark side.

In fifth grade, he would chase Emily at recess, and smack her on the butt with an eraser from the chalkboard. She would scream and run to the safety of the girls' bathroom.

Why the hell did I do that?

When it came to chasing Emily, he had about as much self-control as Larry Talbot did when he turned into the Wolf Man.

A couple of the other boys did it too, but not to Emily. They each had their own girl to chase, but their girls ran much slower. They even laughed as they darted into the girls' bathroom with chalk on their butts.

He could have chased other girls, but it wouldn't have been the same. There was just something about Emily's rear end that made him want to smack it with an eraser. He didn't want to do it; he had to do it—even though she called him names from the safety of the porcelain forbidden zone.

Ozzy never touched Emily's butt with his bare hand, though. One of the boys told him about a guy from some school in

Wisconsin who smacked a girl's butt without any eraser insulation, and his face melted like the Nazis when they touched the lost ark. He was pretty sure it never happened.

As if—but better safe than sorry.

Ozzy tried his best to stop chasing Emily. It wasn't easy. Once, he went four whole days without smacking her behind. For some reason, it only made her meaner.

Why didn't she brush off the chalk marks?

He knew she saw them. She'd look over her shoulder, stick her rump out, and check out the chalk dust. If she knew he was watching, she'd shake her head and glare at him.

Even though Emily was mean to him, he liked knowing the chalk marks were still there. For the rest of the day, every time he saw those white rectangles, he felt a strange bond between them.

He never told his friends about it. He didn't tell them about a lot of things, but it didn't matter. There was no shortage of comics and movies to talk about.

But that was then, and now there was a Valentine's Day card, or whatever it was, to deal with.

My heart bleeds for you, sounds kinda romantic—in a morbid sort of way. Or was she referring to my heart after she plunges a dagger into it. Only one thing to do—open the damn card.

He wondered why the prospect of opening the card made him feel so queasy?

It's just a stupid card.

He scanned the classroom, and opened up the card, half expecting some malevolent spirit would leap out, but there was only a brief inscription inside and some more skulls. It read: *Meet me at Dixon's Donut Shop after school. Come alone. Emily.* Not love Emily, or yours truly Emily—just Emily. It sounded more like a ransom note than a Valentine's Day card.

The more Ozzy tried to divine her intentions, the more bewildered he became. He never considered the possibility a girl as talented and beautiful as Emily would actually be interested in him—in that way.

Even though he had three classes with her, their conversation was pretty much limited to him saying hi, and her responding with an obligatory nod or an exasperated eye roll.

She did stare at him, now and then, but she always looked pissed off. He realized his only hope of solving the mystery was to stop thinking about it and meet her at the damn donut shop.

When Ozzy arrived at Dixon's, he looked in the window. Emily sat alone in a secluded corner of the shop. She stared at a paper bag in the center of the table. Blotchy red stains showed through the white paper.

He began to imagine what was in the bag.

A severed hand, a real heart, a knife, eyeballs, some of those star shaped things ninja's throw.

The list of possible body parts and weapons that would easily fit inside the bag was long, and thinking about it made him nervous.

Emily glanced up at him through the window, and gazed at him with her Wednesday Addams eyes. It was as if she could sense his presence through the glass.

Part of him wanted to bolt, but part of him was hypnotized by her spooky eyes, and wanted nothing more than to look at her all afternoon. He wondered if it was some kind of vampire charm thing. She certainly looked the part.

That can't be it. There's no such thing as vampires. Besides, the sun was out and, she doesn't have the teeth for the job.

Whatever she was doing made his stomach feel like he'd swallowed worms.

I ain't afraid of no girl.

He broke free of Emily's tractor beam gaze, and entered the shop. As he approached her table, she rose, like gravity only partially applied to her.

Emily grabbed her bag, "There you are. Follow me," and hurried into a narrow corridor, toward the restrooms.

Ozzy said, "Hold up. Where are we going?"

She glanced over her shoulder, "You'll see."

He followed a few paces behind. Close enough to breathe

in her heady fragrance. The scent reminded him of clove gum, licorice candy, and the flowers at his Aunt Vivian's funeral.

As they passed the women's restroom, he wondered if she would duck inside, but she didn't.

Ozzy liked the way Emily's hips swayed as she walked. He was relieved he no longer had any desire to smack her butt with an eraser, even though it provided a somewhat larger target than it did in grammar school.

He closed the gap between them. She flung open the iron security door, at the rear of the shop, and glided into the sunshine like a playful spirit.

"C'mon, c'mon," she said.

He bounded outside. The door clanged shut behind him.

Emily took his hand and pulled him into the deserted alley.

"This is the best time of day to see it," she said, "The light is perfect."

Afternoon sunlight bathed the back wall of the donut shop. Ozzy squeezed Emily's hand as he stared in disbelief at a magnificent mural that covered the entire wall.

"I painted that," she said, "It took me all winter break. Got paid too."

He didn't know much about art, but he knew the mural was good enough to be a horror movie poster or box art for a fantasy video game.

The mural featured a totally Goth couple. They stood hand in hand in a moonlit cemetery. Tombstones jutted up at odd angles from a blanket of ethereal fog. Bats hung from the branches of the barren trees, framing the couple on either side. The girl wore a maroon, satin, low-cut dress.

Hey, that looks a lot like Emily—if she had huge anime eyes, with mascara tears.

The boy wore a white, frilly shirt, black leather duster, and riding boots.

Emily scrutinized Ozzy as he scrutinized her mural.

After a long silence, Emily said, "Well, what do you think?"

Ozzy knew he had to say something arty, but didn't know how, so he just said, "Cool."

Not enough verbiage, say something more. Anything. Fast. Ah, fuck it.

Ozzy looked into Emily's eyes and said, "That is one spooky cool, badass, fucking mural, Emily."

She almost smiled and said, "Thanks."

He pointed to the ten-foot tall girl on the wall, "She kinda looks like you."

Emily looked down at her Doc Martens and said, "It is me—if I had bigger boobs."

He almost said he liked her small ones, but stopped himself in time.

He pointed to the guy in the mural, "Who's the dude?"

"Don't you recognize him?" she said.

He cocked his head, "A black Johnny Depp?"

"Not even close," she said.

He held up his hand to hide the big eyes.

Shit. Shit. Shit.

He did recognize the guy.

At the same instant she said, "It's you, silly. I painted it from your yearbook picture."

He looked up at the Goth couple holding hands in the mural, then down at Emily's hand in his. The blood rushed to his brain as he tried to do the math on the Emily conjecture. He'd been doing calculus since the sixth grade, but he sensed the formula necessary to solve this conundrum could only be found in the Twilight Zone.

He remembered feeling this scared and excited once before—waiting in line to ride a roller coaster.

Hope I don't throw up this time.

Emily released her grip on his hand, and turned to face him. He tensed as she reached into the white paper bag.

Okay, here it comes. She's done makin' nice.

"You okay?" she said.

He forced a smile, "Yeah, yeah—I'm good."

She eyed Ozzy with suspicion as she pulled a jelly donut from the bag. He felt like an idiot. Donuts were at the top of his food pyramid, and this was the golden capstone. It was obscenely oversized, deep-fryer fresh, dusted with powdered sugar, and oozing scarlet raspberry jelly. His paranoia turned to avarice in an instant.

The donut looked like a pure white dove in the hands of a bewitching dark angel.

She's so much more beautiful than the girl in the painting.

Emily raised the donut like an offering, and took a bite. Confectioner's sugar rained down on her lacy black blouse. Without thinking, Ozzy started to brush the powder off. Emily pressed his hand on her chest and held it there. He could feel her heart beat quick and strong.

Emily leaned forward and pressed her lips to his. They were soft and warm—and tasted like raspberries.

It was his first kiss and he liked it—a lot.

He ran the tip of his tongue across her raspberry lips—they parted.

Their tongues touched.

A vile taste exploded in his mouth—like rancid fish.

Ozzy's eyes sprang open.

His tongue flopped around in Eaton's slimy mouth like a herring sloshing in a bucket of chum.

The acrid stench of the repulsive maniac seared his nostrils. Ozzy jerked his head so hard he could feel his cervical vertebrae pop like bubble wrap.

The fiend's pursed lips resembled a prolapsed anus with rotting teeth.

The repulsive lunatic made sickening smoochy sounds as he stroked Ozzy's matted hair.

Ozzy started to laugh and cry at the same time.

A sardonic grin spread across Eaton's cadaverous face. The crazed devil leaped from his captive's chest.

Ozzy gasped a lung-full of stale, frigid air.

Eaton circled the perimeter of the tomb-sized, room like a caged beast. He scanned his surroundings, spied the medical kit, and pounced on it. He riffled through its contents, and muttered to himself as he organized an ominous assortment of surgical devices on the floor.

Neat little piles of sterile packages fanned out in a semi-circle at the maniac's feet. Their unwholesome purpose was a mystery to Ozzy, but one thing was certain; whatever it was, it was going to hurt.

An orthopedic saw with sharp, serrated teeth took center stage in the sinister display

Sweat stung Ozzy's eyes. "What're ya gonna do with those, Ben?"

Eaton grabbed the saw.

"What're ya gonna do with that, Ben?"

"You'll see, Mr. Meat. You and your animal protein and your junk food. I know what I know. You like meat? I'll show you meat."

Ozzy thrashed on his urine soaked cot.

Eaton ripped open one of the packages and removed a hypodermic. He rummaged through his supplies, found a bottle of morphine and filled the syringe.

Eaton advanced with the hypo—slobbering—eyes wild. "I want meat, and I want it now."

Ozzy braced himself for the bite of the cold needle and the horror that would surely follow. Ozzy's anus tightened as he stared directly into his tormentor's crazy eyes. He was as ready as any sane man could be to die at the hands of a deranged cannibal.

But instead of jabbing the needle into Ozzy, Eaton plunged the hypodermic into a vein in his own withered arm. The expression on Eaton's pain wracked face softened as the opiate surged to his tortured brain.

He flexed his gangly biceps, threw his head back, and sighed.

A warm wave of ecstasy washed away the pain from every convolution in Eaton's squirming cortex.

Ozzy looked stunned. "What the hell did you do that for?"

"Courage."

"So, you have to get baked before you have the guts to butcher me?"

Eaton looked surprised. "Oh, I'd never eat your tainted

meat. It's poison. Too many preservatives and toxins. I have my own meat, corn-fed, free range, sweet meat."

With that, Eaton grabbed the surgical scissors, snipped his right pant-leg open, and peeled it back.

Tufts of white, fluffy insulation framed his leg. It looked painfully naked in the unnatural light of the flickering television screen. Eaton seized a rubber tourniquet and wrapped it around his emaciated leg—just below his bulbous knee. He thrust his leg out straight, and cinched the tourniquet tight. Eaton grabbed the orthopedic saw and rested the razor-sharp blade across the top of his bony shin. In the hands of a healer, the precision cutting tool would have been an instrument of mercy. In the hands of a maniac, it was the doorway to hell.

Eaton took a deep breath and sawed at an awkward angle. As he ripped the blade back and forth, he yelped like an injured dog. Perspiration poured from his forehead and ran down his chin. It mingled with the crimson puddle that grew larger with every agonizing stroke. Blood spattered the walls and ceiling with each downward thrust. Grizzly globs of gore pelted Ozzy, as he lay helpless, weeping on his cot.

Ozzy screamed for Ben to stop, but his frantic pleas were drowned out when Eaton started humming *It's a Small World*. It was loud and out of tune, but it kept time to the cadence of the blade.

Half way through, the bloody saw jammed in his dense tibia. Eaton stopped and raised his leg enough to take the pressure off the deep, narrow gash. One long backward stroke got him back on track.

The wet, grinding squeal of surgical steel on brittle bone reverberated in Ozzy's spinal cord. He shivered with each rip of the blade.

Eaton had almost cut clean through, when an uncooperative flap of skin at the back of his calf made him stop. He grimaced and wrestled a scalpel from its sterile paper sheath. A few quick slashes detached the twitching appendage. Eaton's scrawny leg rolled over, and plopped into the pond of blood and gristle—cold and slippery like a dead fish. He collapsed—pale and exhausted.

Eaton panted until he caught his breath. As if acting more on some crude instinct than with a conscious sense of purpose, he tucked his lifeless leg under his arm, and scooted backward to the corner of the room. He propped his hunger-ravished carcass against the wall, and positioned his repellent prize in front of him. Eaton hovered over his amputated limb—a predator guarding its kill.

As Ozzy watched his crippled friend, in disbelief, a feeling of profound pity replaced the utter terror he felt only moments earlier.

Ben snarled at Ozzy as he nibbled pulpy, little strips of raw flesh from the mangled stump.

Ozzy stared at the loathsome slab of meat and gristle and shook his head. The horrifying consequences of slow starvation that lay before him weren't nearly as hideous as one pathetic realization. His desperate friend's mutilated appendage was still wearing its thick wool sock and leather snow boot.

Ozzy said, "You coulda taken off your fucking boot, Ben. If I ever get outta here, I'll never be able to watch someone tap their foot to a tune, or kick a football without thinking about your damn leg."

Eaton grunted and kept on eating. He fumbled with the bootlace, but it required too much dexterity and he gave up.

Eaton dragged his severed leg to his lap, reached in his pocket and pulled out the scalpel. He gouged out thick hairy chunks of pink, pulpy flesh and stuffed them into his greedy mouth.

It was painful to watch him gnaw on the meaty hunks, but Ozzy was afraid to look away. There was no telling what his inhuman friend might do next.

Eaton paused occasionally to dislodge clumps of coarse hair from his throat. He hawked them up like a cat with a hairball.

From the television, Ozzy heard, "Antarctica, an angry continent on an angry planet. Earthwatch One, a remote science station at the bottom of the world." He looked over at the TV in time to see himself, Ben and their science station on their Discovery Channel documentary.

Just as it played in the EDI lunchroom—at that exact same moment—a world away.

"Hey Ben, look, we're on TV," Ozzy said.

Eaton kept his eyes on his meat.

"Untie me. We can watch ourselves on television," Ozzy said, "You can sit in the La-Z-Boy."

After devouring more than half of his calf muscle, Eaton pushed his ghastly meal away. He scooted sideways, pulled the radio off a nearby table, and jabbered away for several minutes.

Ozzy had no way of knowing whether Eaton was actually getting through to Marcus in the EDI communication center.

Eaton's face blanched. He dropped the radio and burped. It was a wet rumbling burp that percolated from deep inside his abdomen. His face turned white. Too many weeks had passed since he'd eaten anything—let alone raw meat. One gurgling belch led to another. Eaton's back stiffened, his head jutted forward, his jaw dropped—then it all came up. Undigested bits of his own flesh spewed from his gaping mouth. His frail body convulsed. Bubbling globs of gore covered Eaton. He stared at the suet in his lap and sobbed.

With a violent sideways twist, he dumped his regurgitation on the floor.

Something shiny glistened in the pool of blood and globs of gore.

Eaton fished out the scalpel, clinched it between his teeth, and slithered toward Ozzy like a hideous, maimed lizard.

When he reached the cot, he pulled himself on top of Ozzy and jerked the scalpel under his prisoner's chin.

Ozzy recoiled.

Eaton leered down at his partner and said, "I'm sorry."

Ozzy shut his eyes and gritted his teeth, grateful for any kind of end to his torture.

Swish.

The scalpel whizzed past Ozzy's ear.

Pop, pop, pop.

Ozzy opened his eyes in time to see the nylon cord tumble into curly piles on either side of his cot.

Eaton skulked back to his bloody corner.

Ozzy took a deep breath, stretched, and sat-up.

Eaton clutched the tourniquet around his stump with one hand, and juggled the TV remote with the other.

He zapped through the channels until he found the news and stopped.

Lorelei reported a story about a woman from Charleston, South Carolina who was seriously burned when her micro-waved egg blew up in her face.

Eaton silently mouthed, "I love you." He gazed at Ozzy with watery eyes, and tightened his grip on the tourniquet. "This is no good, Ozzy." Eaton ripped the tourniquet off his mutilated stump. Blood gushed in all directions.

"No!" Ozzy reached out to his friend.

Eaton collapsed in a heap.

Ozzy leaped off his cot, but his legs crumpled under him.

He dragged himself through the blood to his friend. He applied pressure to the stump.

C'mon buddy, you can't die. Not like this.

Felt for a pulse. Nothing. Ben had left the room.

Ozzy slumped down next to his lifeless friend, and gazed up at the television.

Lorelei fiddled with some papers, and said, "This is Lorelei Teller, for Frontline News, good night."

The corner of her mouth rose ever so slightly. For once, Ozzy watched the enigmatic newswoman closely.

She does seem to know more than she was telling.

Ozzy picked up Eaton's half-eaten leg, and unlaced the boot.

His thoughts raced.

Is it even a leg anymore? It can't be used to take a walk in the park, or bounce a baby. Now, it just meat. So, where does the meat leave off and Ben begin?

Ozzy pulled the boot off, and removed the bloody wool

sock.

At what point does the sum total of all the meaty parts add up to something more than sirloin?

If Ozzy were sitting in a coffeehouse, back in the world, sipping espresso with friends, the answer would come easily. In his frozen prison, so far from home, he didn't have a clue.

Ozzy rolled the sock with care, slid it inside the boot, and threw the boot at the wall.

Silence Stalking

Ozzy stretched out on his cot and mindlessly zapped through TV channels. He stopped at the Shopping Network. Two folksy pitchmen, Clyde and Lamar, hawked a neo-medieval knife collection.

Nice beard, Clyde. Is it real? And that camo shirt—if you had any muscles, you'd be wearing a vest.

"I'm gonna toss in one of my favorites, Lamar," Clyde said, "the twenty-six-inch Inquisitor."

Lamar looked shocked. "This is a *Knives at Home* exclusive, folks. Clyde has lost his mind."

It's going to take more than a trucker hat to make that brown suit look country, Lamar.

"You gotta get in on this opportunity at only two hundred and ninety-nine dollars and ninety-five cents," Clyde said, "I'm even throwing in a furniture-grade stand."

Lamar held up a miniature Bowie knife. "Now here's a *Clyde*-sized knife—the Mini Troll."

The TV crew laughed in the background.

Lamar stuck the tiny knife in the big log.

Clyde nodded knowingly. "Well Lamar, as every *real* knife collector knows, it's not the size of your blade, it's how you use it."

Ozzy glared at the television and did something he hadn't done in a long, long time. He turned the television off.

Ozzy tossed the remote on the floor, and folded his arms tight against his chest. Clyde and Lamar receded into a tiny point of light, and the screen went black—so did the room.

Ozzy stared up at the pitch black where the ceiling once was.

The TV had been on twenty-four hours a day for months. When he turned the damn thing off, it was as if he'd bricked up his only window on the outside world. The room was only nine feet wide by twelve feet long. But now it felt smaller— much smaller—more like a cryonic chamber.

The air was thick and heavy. It pressed down on Ozzy's chest. He couldn't take a deep breath, so he bit off bite-sized chunks of air and gulped them into his gasping lungs.

Then came the *silence*. He never noticed it before. Now, he couldn't imagine how something so monstrous could have stayed hidden for so long?

An absorbent stillness enveloped the room and sucked out any trace of sound. Not even an empty echo remained. The silence had been there all along—waiting. The way death waits patiently for that one little slip-up, that one wrong turn—that one last heartbeat.

Ozzy wanted to scream, but could not.

What if I scream and no sound came out? What if the silence rips the scream from my throat and devours it before it reaches my ears?

He tried to move his fingers, but they felt like they belonged to someone else—someone dead. They were rigid. Ozzy stiffened in terror. The ravenous void that surrounded him swallowed the sum total of all he was. The room, his body, Ben's cadaver—it all vanished into the belly of nil minus zero. Only his thoughts remained, and they were even darker than the nothingness that consumed him.

A suffocating panic squeezed Ozzy from all directions. An ominous sense of spiritual dread compacted all that was happy into a dense singularity where the dark entered and no light escaped. It was cold, and silent, and dead. The force of its frozen darkness blew out the gentle flame that burned in the center of his being. Everything that was bright and warm was gone. All that remained was the cold, silent darkness—and the fear.

He lay paralyzed for an eternity of heartbeats. Ozzy had never been afraid of the dark or even death. His terror went far beyond the fear of simple oblivion. It was like he told Ben, if he froze in this barren wasteland, he might have to endure a conscious awareness of the unyielding silence for a billion years. He had only experienced the ghastly void for a few minutes and it was already unbearable.

I'll never enjoy the luxury of natural decomposition. No lush green cemetery for me, or the company and kind attention of worms. I'll simply freeze solid in the sterile ice and remain unchanged until the sun goes super nova, and incinerates the entire fucking solar system. I can't wait that long to be warm again. I can't. I can't. I can't.

Something tepid crept down Ozzy's cheek. The faint drum beat of a single tear tapped on his taut, canvas cot. It was a tiny sound, but nothing ever sounded so sweet. The silence retreated just enough for Ozzy to take a shallow breath.

Ozzy knew exactly what he had to do. There was only one thing noisy enough to keep the silence away for good. He moved one leg, then the other. The dense compression of the room made it almost impossible to move. Ozzy crawled on his hands and knees, patting the floor like a blind man until he found the remote. His hands trembled as he clicked it on. A tiny speck of light in the center of the screen exploded into a cheerful rectangle of vivid color.

The Shopping Channel flashed back on.

A young boy ran through a wildflower meadow. He was only a painting on a porcelain collectors' plate, but he had everything Ozzy wanted. He seemed so content and carefree. He wore tattered overalls with paisley patches, a plaid shirt and black high-top sneakers. A cocker spaniel frolicked at his side. An easy breeze tossed his hair as he flew a homemade kite. Its knotted dishrag tail sketched lazy loops in a watercolor sky. Comfy clouds drifted nowhere in particular above a Norman Rockwell world.

Ozzy could breathe again.

The silence retreated to its hiding places in the cracks and corners.

Everything was the same as before. But now Ozzy knew

that somewhere beyond the wild flower meadows, the hideous silence waited for him to turn off the TV.

The pitch-woman's motherly voice described the limited-edition plate in amazing detail. The camera zoomed in to capture every cheerful brushstroke. It seemed impossible anyone could have so much to say about anything. Ozzy didn't mind. He would have gladly ordered a plate if he had a phone.

The orders rolled in and the soothing voice droned on. Ozzy fell asleep. He dreamed of summer afternoons and soaring kites.

Ozzy awoke to a fast-talking huckster hawking fake diamond rings on the shopping channel. Ozzy watched a cubic zirconium bauble slowly rotate on its clear Lucite base. The Pit was cold, but not that cold. He hadn't shaken the icy feeling of dread that crept into his bones the night before. Ozzy boiled a pot of water and stared down at the rolling bubbles.

There are going to be some changes made around here.

Commando Combat

Light flickered in the stairwell as Ozzy backed up the stairs clenching a waterproof, Mini Maglite in his teeth. He hoisted Eaton's corpse, a step at a time—with the mutilated leg tucked neatly under one arm. When he reached the top, Ozzy dropped Ben's remains on the ice and scanned the ruins. A star, low on the horizon, shined brighter than the rest. It grew larger as a faint whirling sound grew louder. Ozzy sprinted to an open patch in the ruins. A colossal Cougar 100 helicopter approached—low and fast.

Holy shit, I'm going home.

Ozzy waved his flashlight. "Hey, over here."

The chopper's 20-mm guns opened fire and stitched a deadly seam of molten metal in the ice below.

Ozzy dove and rolled out of the line of fire.

The chopper banked for another pass.

What the fuck?

Ozzy ducked behind the scorched remnants of a cinder-block wall.

The chopper hovered and swept the ruins with a searchlight.

Ozzy peered through the twisted rebar. The helicopter landed in an open space amid the ruins. Several commandos leapt out—ninja-style. They spread out, brandishing side arms and tactical flashlights.

Ozzy immediately recognized the intruders' white uniforms and the red wolf patches. They were identical to uniforms worn by the shooters who fired on him and blew up Earthwatch One.

Ozzy bounded inside the gutted lab. The acrid stench of

scorched equipment and spilled chemicals seared his nose and burned his eyes.

Harsh LED beams streamed through gaping fissures in the crumbling walls, casting horrific silhouettes on what remained of the lab's blackened interior.

Ozzy wanted to cough, but feared it would betray his location, so he clenched his teeth and cowered behind an incinerated section of the lab's geodesic roof.

When the commandos passed, the only light that remained was the helicopter's searchlight. Its wide beam provided enough ambient light for Ozzy to survey his surroundings.

Everything was in pieces—and those pieces were in pieces. He spied a scattered trail of laptop keyboard keys.

Shit, looks like drunk Scrabble players got in a fight over a seven-letter word challenge.

The trail of keys led to Ozzy's mangled laptop. The half-melted display glib-globbed over eviscerated green circuitry. He knew it was his laptop because of the Misfits sticker on the case. He used to like the way the grinning skull lit up from the glowing apple underneath.

As Ozzy scanned the senseless destruction surrounding him, his fear turned to anger—then to rage.

Who do these assholes think they are? If they want to take me out, I'm not going to make it easy for them.

Ozzy searched the rubble for something he could use to defend himself.

He crawled over to where the equipment shelving unit should have been. All he could salvage was a dented aluminum case surrounded by twisted Metro shelving that looked like a junk-art sculpture. He popped the latches and found two undamaged, Motorola T80 walkie-talkies inside.

Not much, weapon-wise, but they'll have to do.

He pried one from its black, foam niche.

C'mon, c'mon, work you fucker.

He turned the volume knob—*Click*—The display flashed on.

Yes!

Ozzy turned on the other walkie-talkie and shoved it under a pile of debris in the center of the lab. He ducked under a stainless-steel workbench, clutching the other.

Ozzy hunkered down and waited. Moments later, ice and broken glass crunched nearby.

A single flashlight beam swept the lab. Ozzy crouched lower, watching the lone commando explore the interior of the lab—Glock drawn.

Ozzy held his breath as the intruder approached his hiding place.

Don't look under the table. Nothin' down here. Just move along. Shit, he's going to look under the table. Maybe I could grab his ankles and yank real hard. Then What?

The commando moved closer—close enough to touch.

How the fuck does this guy keep those white combat boots so clean?

The commando pivoted and moved away.

What an idiot. He didn't look under the fucking table. Okay, okay. That's a good thing. An idiot with a gun verses a genius with two walkie-talkies—two walkie-talkies and a plan. I got this.

The hapless commando moved away from Ozzy's table toward some burned out storage lockers. The commando pried opened a twisted, louvered door and pointed his light inside.

Ozzy raised the walkie-talkie to his lips, "Hey, soldier."

The commando pivoted and leveled his gun at the pile of junk where Ozzy had stashed the other walkie-talkie. "Don't shoot. I surrender."

The commando looked confused and kicked the talking debris.

Ozzy rolled out from under the table and sprang to his feet.

The commando whipped around.

Ozzy delivered a sweeping kick.

The gun sailed from the commando's hand.

Ozzy and the commando faced off.

"Okay, who the hell are you guys, anyway?" Ozzy demanded.

The commando charged and delivered a blow to Ozzy's chest. It was the first time anyone hit him in anger. Ozzy was surprised it didn't hurt more, but troubled that it made him feel weak and queasy.

In a heartbeat, a euphoric rage surged through his veins and replaced all traces of weakness. It felt good—too good. The way something bad can feel so good. Of all the things Ozzy ever wanted, in his entire life, he never wanted anything more than to hurt this guy—hurt him good.

The commando showed Ozzy some moves he learned at commando camp.

Ozzy ducked and dodged several punches before demonstrating several kickboxing exercises he learned from Tanya Brown. He couldn't decide where to put his lead elbow, so he just slammed it into the side of the commando's head.

Bowshot—that fucking hurt.

The asshole cried out, and stumbled sideways, grabbing his head with both hands.

Ozzy remembered Tanya always delighted in kneeing the big bag in the groin area, so he did the same.

The commando made a sound Ozzy never heard before, except maybe in a wildlife documentary.

Ya know, if a guy's worth kneeing in the groin once, he's worth kneeing in the groin twice.

The more pain Ozzy inflicted on the commando, the more euphoric he felt. He never wanted the fight to end.

Damn, I'm not going to be able to show this idiot my favorite exercise—the roundhouse kick. Not with him doubled over like that.

Ozzy solved the problem with and old-school uppercut.

The commando flew up and back just long enough for Ozzy to deliver a flawless roundhouse.

Ozzy pivoted on the balls of his left foot, swept high and hard with his right leg. The circular force of Ozzy's shin caught the commando square in the nose.

Blood pinwheeled in all directions. Crimson crystals rained down on Ozzy, stinging his eyes and cheeks.

Icy dust and soot clouded the freezing air when the disoriented commando crumpled to the floor.

The bloody predator crawled on hands and knees to escape his deadly prey.

Ozzy yanked him to his feet. "Going somewhere?"

The kickboxing scientist smeared blood all over the commando's face and dragged him over to a steel beam.

Ozzy shoved his dazed attacker's bloody face onto the frozen metal.

The commando struggled, with his face cemented to the icy beam.

Ozzy let go, and stepped back to admire his work. "If I'm not mistaken, the only way to get you unstuck is to—"

"Just do it. Piss on my face," The commando said, in a thick, French-Canadian accent.

"Hey, we just met. Chat me up a little first."

"Okay, okay."

"*Sooo*—what do you do for a living?"

"I am a capitaine, monsieur."

"Ah, a military man. Army, Navy—Snow Patrol?"

"No."

"What then?"

"L'ordre Du Loup Rouge."

"What the hell is that?"

"The Order of the Red Wolf. Now piss on my face."

The commando's free eye glared at Ozzy.

"Not so fast. Is that some wacko paramilitary group?"

"We are defenders of our race and Western civilization."

"Defending it from what?"

"The likes of you."

"Environmental scientists?"

"You know what I mean."

I'll bet there's more of him at home.

"Just piss on my face."

I wish your friends could hear you say that.

Ozzy crossed his heart. "I promise I will piss on your face, but I have a few more quick questions."

The commando moaned and squirmed on the beam.

Ozzy continued, "Two of your friends blew up our science station and tried to waste my partner and me. Now why the fuck did they want to go and do that?"

Voices and footsteps echoed in the ruins outside.

Oh shit.

The commando spoke out the side of his mouth, "We do not abide nosy neighbors, mon ami."

"Well neighbor, wasn't that a nuke in *your* backyard, next to the barbecue?"

"Oui, oui, oui. Now, piss on my face."

"Just as soon as I find your fancy pistola."

Ozzy scanned the lab.

Rip.

Scream.

Ozzy whipped around. Half of the capitaine's face was still stuck to the beam, but he was gone.

Where the hell did he go?

Glass crunched behind Ozzy. He pivoted.

The mercenary whipped out a seven-inch tactical knife from his leg sheath and lunged at Ozzy.

Ozzy dodged a clumsy swipe of the blade, and then another.

If this guy's intention is to slash the air to pieces, he's doing a fine job.

It was obvious the guy could barely see through the blood shrouding his eyes. Especially since blinking was no longer an option for the big, round eyeball that gyrated in its naked socket.

Ozzy could barely look at his attacker. He had studied human anatomy, but never this up close and personal. With no eyelids, or nose, or cheek on the left side of his face, the capitaine could have posed for a Famous Monsters of Filmland cover painting.

Ozzy feared his flailing adversary would stab him by accident, so he grabbed the commando's arm.

Ozzy was no expert in hand-to-hand combat, but he'd seen enough action movies to know that if you twisted the bad guy's arm back far enough it would—

Snap.

In real life, the sound of an arm breaking was somewhat muffled compared to the big screen, but the wet crack and the ripping of the meaty parts that followed was far more cringe-worthy.

The knife dropped to the floor, and so did the incapacitated capitaine.

Ozzy picked up the flashlight. "Gotta hand it to you paramilitary ass-hats, you have some pretty cool shit. This is one fine, fine flashlight." He shined it under the examination table. "Where the hell is your damn gun? Watch, it'll be in the last place I look."

The commando whimpered.

Ozzy turned to look.

The capitaine had crawled over to the steel beam, and was trying to peel his face off the icy metal. He sobbed, "Maman, my face, my face."

"Zip it. I'm trying to concentrate," Ozzy said.

"Mongrel, monkey man—look what you have done to my most handsome face."

"I'm not gay, but you did have pretty sweet Arian look goin' there."

You are a sub-human brute. You have taken my only face from me."

"Hey, man—this is all on you. Gotta hand it to you, though. For a man in your condition, you're one chatty motherfucker."

The Commando tried to pry his nose from the beam.

"Yeah, too bad about that beautiful nose. Wish I had a perfect nose like that. Oh wait, I still got my nose—never mind."

Ozzy scanned the lab. "Now, where the fuck is that damn gun?"

Three more commandos stormed the lab.

These guys know where their guns are. They're fucking pointed straight at me.

They grabbed Ozzy and helped their defaced friend to his feet. He howled as one of his comrades tried to hoist him by his bad arm.

A perverse glee burned inside Ozzy's belly as he watched the capitaine's broken arm flop around at odd angles. This new propensity for violence shocked and confused him. Part of him wanted to tell the capitaine he was sorry, but instead he said, "I can piss on your face *now*, mon ami."

Ozzy didn't feel afraid as they hauled him away. His adrenalin buzz was still going strong.

Perfect, more assholes. How can I hurt these new guys? I got it! Start by pissing them off.

"Hey, guys, do you always bring your mothers along on dangerous missions?"

The commando helping his wounded friend said, "What you talkin' 'bout, boy?"

"You're not Canadian." Ozzy said.

"Fuck you, Buckwheat. I'm from Abilene, but we come from all over the damn world—even Russia."

The commando wrangling Ozzy said, "Damnit, Earl, don't tell him our business."

"Don't matter, Jessie. Sambo here ain't long for this world," said Earl.

"Sorry Earl. The only reason I asked is that your friend here has been callin' for his mother. I sure hope she's here. Somebody's gotta change his poopy pants."

Jessie bellowed something indecipherable and shoved Ozzy hard.

As he tumbled to the ice, Ozzy delivered a sweeping kick and brought Jessie down with him. They wrestled for Jessie's Glock.

Pop. Pop. Pop.

A stray bullet entered the capitaine's neck and lodged in Earl's left shoulder.

Earl screamed and dropped the capitaine. He fired at Ozzy. The bullet hit Jessie instead.

Blood spurted from a nine-millimeter hole in Jessie's cheek for a few beats, then slowed to a trickle when his heart stopped pumping.

Before Earl had a chance to fire again, Ozzy grabbed

Jessie's hand with his Glock still in it and managed to squeeze off a single round.

One was enough. Earl's white uniform instantly turned red where his right kneecap used to be.

Earl wailed and grabbed his knee.

Ozzy pried the Glock from Jessie's hand and leveled it at Earl, but he didn't fire. His blood lust had vanished. He had absolutely no desire to fire again.

Ozzy rolled Jessie over and struggled to his feet. He picked up Earl's gun and just stood there, a Glock in each hand, staring down at another human being writhing in agony. Ozzy felt numb and empty, as if some primal entity had possessed him, then abandoned him for some other scared and angry soul.

Before Ozzy had a chance to figure out what to do next, several commandos surrounded him—Uzis at the ready.

Ozzy let the Glocks fall from his hands and raised his arms. "You got me. I surrender."

The commandos charged Ozzy, wrestled him to his knees and dragged him toward the helicopter. The toes of his boots scraped the ice.

I could walk, but fuck it, I am a little tired. Let these idiots work for it.

As they neared the helicopter, Ozzy could see a small steel-eyed man wearing a dressy white military uniform, reclining on a couch. Dr. No would have approved of the decor. The spacious cabin's interior was a designer's overwrought exercise in white on white. The odd little man balanced a platter of sardines and gourmet crackers on his lap. A cadre of his commandos stood at attention on either side of the open door.

Okay, this motherfucker must be the grand wack-job.

One commando held a heavy-duty, chain leash, with a huge dog tethered to the other end. They sat at attention and scrutinized Ozzy as he approached.

Ozzy almost laughed when this savior of Western civilization exited the helicopter like a head of state, sardine platter in hand. The odd, little man, with his white uniform and big pith helmet, struck a heroic pose as if he was going to have his portrait painted.

The little boss scratched the canine's head.

The beast snarled.

"Nice dog." Ozzy said.

The man sneered and shook his head, "That is not a dog, imbecile. Do you not know a wolf when you see one?"

"Oh, I get it," Ozzy pointed to the red, wolf logo on the helicopter, "He's like a mascot—cool."

"This is no sporting team."

"Yeah, yeah," Ozzy gestured to the whimpering captaine, "Your guy, over there, filled me in. You in charge here?"

Oui, oui, I am Colonel Jean-Claude Pomeroy, supreme commander of L'ordre Du Loup Rouge."

"Are you Canadian?"

"I will ask the questions here, but no, I am Belgian."

"Sorry, Sorry, but just out of curiosity, why colonel? If you're the head guy, why not president, or premiere, or at least general?"

"I chose to honor my rank in the Belgian Army."

"Okay, okay. That makes sense—not.

"Now, may I know your name, S'il vous plaît?" the colonel said, as he slurped down a sardine.

"Dr. Ozioma Pratt." Ozzy saluted, "Environmental Defense International." Ozzy couldn't keep his eyes off the sardine platter.

A loud *screech* reverberated through the ruins.

"You have taken the lives of two of my men. They were not my best men, but they were mine, and now you will pay."

"Technically, I didn't kill anybody. Jessie shot the capitaine by accident, I might add. Earl killed Jessie, again by accident. Now, I did shoot Earl in the knee. That was on purpose, but he was trying to kill me."

"No matter. I am going to afford you the honor of dying for your cause, docteur."

"No causes here, but if you're going to kill me, can I at least have a last wish?"

"We are all civilized men here—unlike your savage kind. I will grant your request. A cigarette, perhaps?"

"I don't smoke, but those sardines look pretty good."

Excellent choice, docteur. These are Matiz Gallego. I have them flown in at great expense from Spain. You may have one sardine."

"Do I get a cracker with that?"

"Oui, oui, but just the one."

Ozzy's handlers escorted him to the colonel.

He lifted the becrackered sardine from the platter with all the gentility of a socialite at a cocktail party. Ozzy took a dainty nibble, and rolled his eyes in delight. "This sardine is divine, colonel. Your taste in tiny fish is evidence of a cultured palate." Ozzy finished the hors d'oeuvre with gusto. "Thank you so much colonel, now I can die a happy man."

"Have another, docteur."

"I wouldn't want to impose."

"No, no, I insist."

Screech.

This time it was louder and closer—much closer.

Ozzy smiled and helped himself to another sardine. He wanted to wolf it down—along with all the others, but he took the smallest bites possible to buy time.

"Finish it," the colonel said.

His commandos raised their weapons.

A mutant penguin waddled toward the group, sniffing the air.

"What do we have here?" the colonel said.

Ozzy grinned. "Oh—ah, he's my pet penguin. Say hello to Snapper."

"Odd looking bird, wouldn't you say?"

"Yeah, but he just *loves* people."

The colonel dangled a sardine in front of the slobbering bird.

The freak snapped the sardine and four of the colonel's fingers.

Ozzy laughed as the creature tossed its head back and the colonel's digits disappeared down its gullet.

The colonel screamed and held up his hand, as if showing it to his men would somehow make it all better.

His stunned commandos blasted the ravenous monstrosity as more mutants converged.

As Ozzy inched backward, he snatched up sardines from the ice and stuffed them into his mouth. "It's been great chatting with you guys, but I really should be heading home now," Ozzy said with his mouth full. He broke free and hauled ass for the stairwell. He took a moment to look over his shoulder. The mutants encircled the colonel and his men.

The commandos fired wildly, as the vicious swarm ripped through their clean, white uniforms, devouring the hot, red flesh inside.

The helicopter's searchlight illuminated the feeding frenzy like harsh limelight on a gory Grand Guignol stage.

For the moment, Ozzy was in the clear.

He stopped to catch his breath and watched the surviving commandos drag the colonel's mangled body into the helicopter.

Some of the snapping monstrosities managed to hop inside before the door slid shut.

The sweat on Ozzy's forehead froze. He wiped off the frozen crystals and trudged toward Eaton's corpse and the stairwell, twenty yards ahead.

The chopper's turbine engines roared above the shrill screeches of the mutants and the sickening screams of the commandos.

Ozzy turned for one last look. The cadence of the blades quickened to a steady throb. Rotor wash blew mutants away in all directions as the chopper lifted off.

That's right, you better run—back to your death star, or where ever you evil fucks live. The force is fucking strong in this one.

Ozzy's moment of triumphant bravado turned into blind panic as the colonel's chopper fled into the frigid gloom.

Without its searchlight, Ozzy could see absolutely nothing.

The stairwell was only a few yards away, but it might as well have been on the dark side of the moon.

Ozzy stumbled around in the pitch black, trying to get his

bearings. He'd already been on the ice for far too long. If he didn't find the stairwell soon, he would certainly freeze.

Ozzy patted his parka pockets, in search of his Maglite—nothing. He rifled his snow-pants pockets—lint, ChapStick—nothing else.

Shit. Musta dropped my Maglite when I dove for cover. If I only knew how to navigate by the stars.

Ozzy laughed to himself.

Yeah, like that would do a lot of good. Can't even see the North Star this far south. Down here, every direction is fucking north.

Off in the distance, the screeching mutants seemed to be getting closer. It reverberated off the ruins of Earthwatch One, making it impossible to determine the exact distance or direction of the advancing horde.

Ozzy's guts roiled with a mounting sense of dread. He would have shit if he had any shit to shit, so he peed a little instead.

Damn, why did I do that? I can't see them, so they can't see me—but I'll bet they can smell urine a mile away. Gotta get outta here.

Ozzy stumbled in the dark, arms outstretched like Frankenstein's monster.

An eerie howl resounded on the distant ice. The howling intensified, punctuated by an occasional yelp.

That's the wolf. The colonel's fucking wolf, no doubt. Mutant penguins, and now a wolf. What next, zombies, vampires—Skeletor?

Without thinking, Ozzy dashed off, until—*thuack.* He ploughed headlong into something architectural. He crumpled to the ice and blacked out.

Carrot Cake and Canis Lupus Rufus

When Ozzy came to, frozen drool caked his thick beard. As he chipped off the ice, he noticed a shimmering glow only a few feet away. He crawled over to the mysterious light source. His missing Maglite flickered in a green puddle next to a ruptured antifreeze canister. Ozzy snatched it up and wiped off the green slush that kept the batteries from freezing.

He cupped it in his gloved hands and blew on it, hoping to rekindle the fading ember. When the batteries warmed up, the beam shined brighter.

Ozzy swept the LED beam across the ghostly ruins.

Eaton's frozen corpse lay only a few yards away, and just beyond that, was the yawning entrance to the stairwell. The infernal screeching was closer now and so was the howling.

Ozzy pointed his flashlight in the direction of the screeching.

Just beyond the parameter of the debris field, the wolf bounded straight for him. The swift canine was several wolf-lengths ahead of the mutant penguins, but a mob of the monstrosities converged from either side. They were sure to swarm the powerful beast.

Ozzy dashed to Eaton's corpse and dragged it to the stairwell. He trained his flashlight back at the wolf. Something trailed behind the loping beast. The hand and forearm of the wolf's keeper skipped across the ice, tethered to the wolf's choke-chain leash. Ozzy felt an unexpected kinship with the wolf. The apex predator reminded him of his German Shepard Chewie and the way he'd run to him when he got home from school.

Ozzy waved his flashlight.

Over here, c'mon, c'mon. You can make it.

The mutants converging from either side were now in position to cut the wolf off.

Shit. He's not going to make it. Fuck this.

Ozzy grabbed the only weapon he could find—Ben's frozen leg. It was rock hard and would have to do. He charged toward the mutant horde. He couldn't see the wolf, but he saw plenty of bloody mutants flying in all direction.

Ozzy swung the meat-club, bludgeoning the mutants two and three at a time. He beat a path toward the sound of vicious snarling until the wolf was in view.

The wolf held his own with the frenzied creatures, but he was surrounded—with more mutants on the way.

Ozzy was awestruck by the wolf's ferocity. The beast ripped the creature's throats out and flung them out of the way.

Ozzy cleared a path to the stairwell and hauled ass to Eaton's corpse. He pulled the frozen cadaver onto the first step. He could still hear snarling and yelping, a few feet away.

Ozzy pointed his light.

The wolf held his ground, giving Ozzy time to escape.

Holy shit. You have my back, don't ya? You magnificent, vicious, motherfucker.

Ozzy ripped off a glove with his teeth, shoved his thumb and forefinger in his mouth and whistled. It was one of those whistles his friend could hear from two blocks away when he was playing video games in his bedroom. It was even louder because the stairwell functioned as an echo chamber. It was so loud, in fact, the mutants stopped screeching.

All eyes were now on Ozzy—and there were thousands of them.

The wolf's ears perked up and it charged straight for the stairwell.

Ozzy took advantage of the break in the action. He clinched the Maglite in his teeth and pulled Eaton's frozen cadaver down the stairs—*ump-ump, ump-ump, ump-ump.*

One of the mutants held tight to the wolf-keeper's severed appendage and was dragged with it down the stairs. As the mutant passed Ozzy, it was impossible to tell where the tendons and veins of the commando's hand ended and the creature's noodly tentacles began.

Fucking avian cephalopod freaks.

The wolf tripped on the tangled chain, slid down the stairs and careened into the empty storage drum at the bottom.

Ozzy fumbled with the wolf's choke collar. "Okay, easy boy. Take it easy. You won't be needing this anymore."

The dazed beast held still long enough for Ozzy to remove the collar. When he did, the little monster waddled up the stairs, nibbling on its gory prize.

Ozzy bludgeoned the mutant with his friend's leg, kicked the door open, and lugged Eaton's corpse into the pit.

The wolf leaped inside.

Ozzy slammed the door, set Eaton's corpse down on its cot and positioned the mangled leg reverently across the cadaver's chest.

"Don't worry Ben, I'm not gonna put you outside in the cold again. You can rot right here on your own cot."

Ozzy pulled a canvas tarp over Eaton's ghastly remains. He kept one eye on the wolf.

Ozzy flopped down hard onto his DIY La-Z-Boy, cranked the lever and ratcheted back into happy horizontality, ready for blast off—but with nowhere to go. He fished around the seat cushions and snagged the TV remote. The scientist-turned-berserker's hand shook so hard he could barely push the buttons. He told himself he was shaking from the cold, but he knew better. Ozzy channel surfed and tried to catch his breath, as he pondered what to do about the wolf. The panting beast circled the perimeter of the Pit, and curled up beside the door.

"Well buddy, I'm no expert, but I know wolves come in two flavors, gray and red. Even if you weren't covered with mutant blood, I could see you're a red wolf. Canis Lupis Rufus, if I'm not mistaken. Less than a hundred of you left in the wild."

The wolf rested his head on his front paws and stared at Ozzy.

"How the hell did that maniac Pomeroy get his hands on you? Thanks for the help out there, Rufus. Hope you don't mind if I call you Rufus. Technically, it *is* your name."

The wolf's ears perked up for an instant.

"If only one of us makes it out of here alive, I kinda wish it were you. Last time I checked, science geeks aren't on the endangered species list, at least not yet."

As Ozzy spoke, the wolf rested his head on his front paws and went to sleep.

Ozzy envied the wolf's ability to nod off so effortlessly. There was a time, not so long ago, when he could quiet his mind when things got too crazy. He hadn't meditated since college, but maybe it would help him calm down now. If nothing else, it might keep his heart from pounding so hard and fast.

Ozzy closed his eyes. His mantra started up on its own, as if he'd never stopped meditating. The recurrent rhythm of the silent word-sound kept pace with his racing thoughts. Together, they dove deep toward the familiar, violet glow that throbbed at the boundary that separated the material world from parts unknown. Back when Ozzy meditated regularly, there were times his mind crossed over into an endless sea of bliss. More often than not, there was only the sweet oblivion of lost time—a little death that provided a few moments total peace.

A strong, musky odor wafted into Ozzy's consciousness. He didn't want to open his eyes, but he forced himself.

The piercing, amber eyes of the wolf stared into his. The beast's head rested on his chest. Its huge paws flanked either side of his head. If he hadn't been meditating, Ozzy would have certainly bolted in surprise, if not total panic. Instead, he gazed back at Rufus with the fleeting serenity that lingers for the first few minutes after meditation.

Ozzy could see no death in the wolf's eyes, only curiosity and something else—something behind the eyes of the predator. There were mysteries Ozzy had experienced at the deeper levels of consciousness he never understood. Of one thing, he was certain. Way, way down, past the boundary of the violet glow, somehow, everything was connected—him, the wolf, the TV, a rock on the moon. Had Ozzy and the wolf connected on a deeper level?

Ozzy squinted at the wolf with suspicion. "Okay, nobody hates mystical shit more than me, but did you just jack my meditation, Rufus? Are we, like, hooked up on some cosmic level now?"

Rufus remained motionless and didn't break his gaze.

"Stop looking at me like that. I read somewhere you're not supposed to make eye contact with a wolf. It makes 'em mad. You mad?"

Rufus remained calm, but focused.

"You don't look mad."

A curious sense of knowing resided in the Wolf's gaze.

"Wait a minute, you're not some Buddha wolf, are you?"

Rufus blinked.

"Ah ha—you blinked. Does that mean I'm supposed to solve one of those one hand clapping riddles?" Ozzy closed his eyes, eager for some kind of inter-species telepathy. "Okay, lay it on me."

Nothing.

Ozzy opened his eyes.

The wolf stared back.

"Maybe you're a werewolf. Naw—there was no moon. Shape-shifter, perhaps?"

Rufus yawned.

"Holy shit—what big fucking teeth you have. I got it. It's like that Native American thing. You're my spirit animal, right?"

Rufus cocked his head.

"That's it, then. You're my spirit animal. Whatever the fuck that means."

The wolf reared up.

"Whoa. Okay, ah, Pratt's law, rule number one, a spirit animal does not eat its spirit human."

Rufus put his paws on the headrest of the La-Z-Boy.

"Rule number two—same as rule number one."

Something warm and wet dripped down Ozzy's neck—blood. He grabbed the lever, and the La-Z-Boy sprung to and upright position. The wolf leaped to the floor. Ozzy patted his neck and shoulder—no bites. Rufus slunk toward the door, favoring his right front leg. Droplets of blood trailed behind.

Damn, they got him. He's wounded. A wounded wolf. Great. I'm alone with a wounded spirit animal with no food and no way out of this frozen crypt. What could possibly go wrong?

Ozzy eased off the La-Z-Boy and approached the wolf, talking low and slow. "All right, rule number three, when a spirit animal is ripped to shit by mutant penguins, the spirit human will determine the extent of the injuries."

Ozzy got down on his hands and knees and crawled over to Rufus. A three-inch gash in the wolf's right leg trickled blood. Ozzy lifted the leg with care and examined the wound more closely.

"Could be worse, Rufus. It's pretty deep, but no major arteries or tendons were severed."

Ozzy placed his fingertips on the wolf's broad cranium, hoping to achieve a Vulcan mind meld. "Here's the dealio, Rufus. I'm going to have to close that wound—no way around it." Ozzy glanced over at Eaton's cot. "See the dead guy over there, under the tarp? He used to do this kinda shit, but he's seriously indisposed, so I'm going to do it. Do you understand?" Ozzy made the wolf's head go up and down. "Good, good, let's get started."

Ozzy hopped up and grabbed the medical kit. He lugged it back to Rufus, and popped the lid. "Don't look in the box, Rufus. Trust me, there's some scary shit in there."

The wolf actually turned his head away as if he understood.

Ozzy picked up the bottle of morphine.

If I give this wolf a shot of morphine, it might knock him out and patching him up will be easy-peasy—or he could go all Animal Planet on me.

Ozzy put the morphine back in the box, and grabbed a syringe and a bottle of Novocain.

He filled the syringe with the local anesthetic and lifted the wolf's leg.

"You might feel a little pinch."

Or it might hurt like hell and you'll rip my fucking throat out.

Ozzy stuck the needle in.

Rufus yelped.

"C'mon, now, who's the big bad wolf? You guys will chew your leg off if it gets caught in a trap. This is just a little needle prick."

He held the syringe up for the wolf to see.

Rufus flashed a toothy snarl accompanied by a guttural growl.

"Rule number four, the spirit animal will refrain from growling during medical procedures."

Rufus turned his head away.

"Hey, you look at me when I'm talkin' to you."

The wolf glanced up, then looked down at the floor.

"Wish I had my damn cell. I'd take a photo of you and post it. A wolf looking sheepish. Now that's something you don't see every day."

Ozzy injected the Novocain around the gash in a few more places. He snipped the fur from around the wound with surgical scissors and sutured as best he could. Rufus rested his head on the cold floor and held perfectly still.

"G'boy. That's more like it. Almost done."

Ozzy tied off the last suture, slathered antibiotic all around the wound, and bandaged the wolf's leg with sterile gauze.

Ozzy lifted the wolf's leg. "Not bad."

Rufus rose and limped to the bathroom.

Ozzy followed. "Nothin' for you in there."

The wolf stuck his head in the toilet bowl and recoiled.

"Ah, a toilet drinker. Guess the colonel didn't have a chemical toilet. Hold on."

Ozzy filled his Storm Trooper cereal bowl with water from the bathroom sink. "Chewie always drank from the toilet. It drove me crazy."

Ozzy set the bowl down in front of the TV and plopped down on the La-Z-Boy.

Rufus limped over to it, and lapped away as Ozzy talked.

"When I complained to my mother about Chewie's disgusting drinking habit, she just laughed and said dogs like the cool, toilet water—and the taste. How the hell would she know? I never brought it up again. One time, when Chewie wouldn't eat some new dog food the vet recommended, my mother tasted it to show him how delicious it was. She really hammed it up. She made it look so good I took a big bite. I spit it out immediately and rinsed my mouth out, but I could taste that shit for hours. I never knew for sure if my mother actually liked the taste of the dog food, or if it was all for show. I always wondered about that, but I was afraid to ask her. Years later, I learned the truth. Back when I was still at Caltech, I was in this health food store on Lake Street in South Pasadena."

Rufus looked up at Ozzy.

"I know, I know, I don't look like a health food guy. I'm not. Big believer in supplements, though. Anyway, I'm walking down the center aisle, and this earth goddess in a tie-dye apron waves me over to her card table and hands me this bite-size sample of carrot cake. Now, I love carrot cake and the half-cut cake on the table looked fucking perfect. Creamy cream cheese frosting, a little carrot on top, grated carrots, chopped walnuts. It even had real pineapple bits. Not those damn yellow raisins. So, imagine my surprise when I popped the sample in my mouth, and it tasted like Chewie's prescription dog food. I didn't want to hurt the nice girl's feelings, so I pretended to swallow. I tried like hell not to gag. I think she confused my shocked expression for curiosity because she beamed and announced the carrot cake was 100% gluten free. Don't get me wrong, Rufus, I got nothin' against gluten free food. Some of my A-list foods don't have any fucking gluten. French fries—gluten free. Tacos—nada. Ice cream. Even Cheetos are gluten free, for fuck's sake. This wasn't about simply taking gluten out of something. I don't know what the pretty hipette put in her carrot cake instead of gluten, but whatever it was tasted like ass. Artisanal donkey ass or somethin'. Yeah, that's it, she replaced the gluten with ass. I had to spit that shit the fuck out, so I faked a smile and ducked down the herbal tea aisle. It was almost too late. My cheeks were really poofing out. I couldn't fucking swallow, so saliva was building up. That carrot-ass-cake was turning into mulch in my mouth. There was no time to try and find a bathroom, so I grabbed one of those reusable shopping bags with the store logo on it and spit the gluten free ass cake sludge into it. I could still taste it, so I sidestepped this healthy-looking sweater guy who'd been leering at me the whole time and headed for the refrigerated beverage aisle. I'm not juice savvy, so I just grabbed a bottle of cranberry juice and took a big gulp. Lemme tell ya, that shit was fucking sour. There isn't even a word for how sour that shit was. I looked at the label—UNSWEETENED CONCENTRATE. Some rogue, Montsanto botanist with a DARPA grant weaponized those cranberries. My face musta looked pretty fucking scary because this hipster, wearing *Kill Bill* yellow, yoga pants took one look at me and hustled his lumpy butt toward the raw nut bins. My whole face made a beeline for my nose to escape the sour-agedon through my nostrils. My eyes were all squinty, but I could still make out a gaggle of teens, snapping photos of me with their phones. My sour-puss is bound to turn up as a meme, some day."

Ozzy scrunched up his face and so did Rufus.

"The taste of ass cake was gone, but I had an idea. I bought a whole carrot cake and took it to my mother. My parents only lived forty-five minutes away in the Miracle Mile. It wasn't weird that I dropped by. I went home every couple of weeks to do laundry and have some of my mother's rice. Anyway, I gave her the carrot cake. She made a big deal about it, even put it on a silver serving plate. Now, most Nigerian food is totally delicious, but they eat some weird-ass shit, like mopani worms. They're actually these colorful caterpillars. They look like fancy hard candy. So, if she liked the gluten fucking free carrot cake, then I'd know if she really liked the way dog food tasted. Don't ask me why I needed to know. I just did. It was one of those dumbass kid things."

Ozzy got up from the La-Z-Boy and paced as he talked.

Rufus followed him, favoring his wounded leg.

"So, she cut a piece of cake, took a bite, and acted like she liked it. Big smile and all. Then she scurried off to the kitchen. I followed her and peeked through the swinging door. She spit the ass cake out in the sink and washed her mouth out with water from the faucet. I never saw her drink out of the faucet before. She hated that fucking cake as much as me."

Ozzy started to sob. He dropped to his knees and looked Rufus straight in the eye. He could barely talk.

"My mother ate prescription dog food because if Chewie didn't, he'd die. He wouldn't eat it, and he did die, Rufus. He died in my fucking arms. The vet brought him in the examining room with an IV in his foreleg, and put him on the cold metal table."

Ozzy put his arms around Rufus' neck and sobbed into the wolf's thick fur.

"I held on to Chewie. I held him tight. Like this. He was breathing heavy. I told him it was going to be all right, but it wasn't all right. I lied. The last thing I told him was a lie. I could have said I love you or even goodbye, but no, I told him it was going to be all right. The vet released this pink liquid into the IV, and Chewie just stopped breathing. That was it. No final gasp. No death spasm. He didn't even close his eyes. My mother cried—hard. I didn't cry. I was too mad to cry. She cried all the way home with Chewie's favorite blanket wadded up in the back seat of the Volvo. I kept that blanket under my bed for years. It still had some of his fur on it. It smelled like him for a long time. Eventually his scent faded. I hadn't thought of him since college and the damn carrot cake. Thanks for making me finally work that shit out."

Ravenously Rufus

Days passed, but the gnawing hunger of man and beast did not. As Rufus grew more and more restless, Ozzy could not imagine any good end to their relationship. He even tried to get his canine roommate to eat Ben's remains, but the wolf showed no interest in the tarp covered cot and the carrion it contained. When Rufus began scratching at the door, Ozzy realized it was time for him to go.

"I hear ya, buddy. You need to find a dignified end in nature. I won't forget you. As if I'm going to be around long enough forget anything."

Ozzy unbolted the door, knelt next to Rufus and whispered in the Wolf's ear, "Love ya, man. I'm not going to lie to you like I did to Chewie. I'm not telling you it's going to be all right. This situation is about as fucking far from being all right as a situation can get."

Ozzy pulled the door open. "Go on, get the fuck outta here."

The sub-zero wind rushed in as Rufus bounded up the icy steps. The wolf stopped at the top of the stairs, looked down at Ozzy for a long moment, then ran off into the cold unknown. Ozzy stared into the black oblivion of the endless polar night until the cold forced him inside. The solitary survivor pushed the door closed, leaned against it as he snapped the bolt closed, and faced the tarp-covered cot.

"Fuck you, Ben, I'm not giving you the satisfaction of seeing me cry. He was a wolf, okay. Rufus wasn't Chewie. He was a wild animal. There's no such thing as spirit animals or a Buddha wolf, Ben. So just forget about it."

Ozzy made it to his recliner without even misting up a little bit. As he sat down and reached for the remote, a wailing cry echoed on the distant ice.

Must be the wind or some lost soul in the freezing abyss.

Ozzy felt a hand on his shoulder. He turned, and it was Ben. The sad-faced apparition said, "You know, full well that's Rufus out there."

Ozzy said, "Is Rufus trying to say goodbye?"

Ben said, "No, Ozzy. The wolf is saying it's going to be all right."

Another howl rose with lonesome sustain and trailed off to a plaintive cry.

"How do you know?" Ozzy said as he stared at the door.

"I know what I know."

Ozzy turned back to his friend, but Ben was gone.

Destination Deepfreeze

"Next up, a live report from the Earthwatch One rescue expedition." A logo flashed on the TV screen: DESTINATION DEEPFREEZE.

Ozzy bolted for the television.

They cut to Lorelei wearing a tailored parka. "I'm coming to you live from Christchurch, New Zealand, a thousand miles north of the frozen continent of Antarctica. For some, it's the last frontier, a land of frigid beauty and adventure. But when the murderous Antarctic wind rips down the immense south polar ice dome and slashes across the vast frozen desert like a thousand maniacs, adventure can end in a cold and lonely grave." Eaton and Ozzy's PR photos filled the TV screen. "If all goes well, we will witness the rescue of two brave scientists, Dr. Benjamin Eaton and Dr. Ozioma Pratt."

Ozzy sprang from the La-Z-Boy and knelt in front of the TV.

Lorelei continued, "With me now is Frank Sayer, leader of the Earthwatch One rescue expedition. Mr. Sayer, what are the chances these men are still alive?"

Sayer adjusted the bandage on his injured tongue and said, "Environmental Defenth International provided them with the motht thophisticated thience thtation on the continent and a yearth worth of food."

"When do you plan to attempt the rescue?"

"If the weather holdth, we thould reach Earthwatch One in a few dayth."

Ozzy tapped the TV screen.

That's Terra in the background. Ho-ly-shit. Terra. Is that really you?

"We'll have more as this story unfolds. Now back to our studios in Atlanta." Lorelei signed off with her signature smirk.

Ozzy looked over at Eaton's tarp covered cot. "Did you hear that, Ben? We're goin' home."

Ozzy took deep breaths and turned on the hotplate.

A cup of hot water might calm me the fuck down. Shit. Now, I really gotta pee.

He trotted into the bathroom and screwed in the bare bulb dangling overhead. He caught a glimpse of himself in the medicine cabinet mirror.

Terra can't see me like this. I look like a Bob Marley-zombie-werewolf.

The kettle whistled. Instead of pouring the boiling water in his crusty cup, he emptied the whole pot into his Storm Trooper bowl. He found some scissors, soap, a razor and went to work. The hot water felt good on his cold face and hands. First, he washed his long greasy dreadlocks, and tied them back in a ponytail. Then he scrubbed, lathered and shaved.

The transformation was astounding. He turned his head from side to side, in disbelief.

Well, who the hell are you?

The guy in the mirror mouthed his words, but it wasn't him. It wasn't Ozzy the hulking, too tall blimp. It wasn't the same Ozzy who was always the last one picked for any team sport in grammar school—but it was.

The only features he could recognize were his eyes. Actually, only the irises looked the same. They were still gray-brown, but his puffy bags were gone and so were his fleshy eyelids.

Something seemed different about his nose. It used to look too small, sandwiched between his massive cheeks. Now, it was just the right size. Ozzy marveled at the sight of cheekbones. He'd never seen them before. They were high and angular. And he had only one chin instead of three. It was strong and broad and looked like it could take a punch. He ran his hands over the contours of his new face, laughed and unscrewed the light bulb.

~

The next day, Ozzy straightened up the Pit with renewed fervor. He glanced at the TV. A mother sniffed her baby's head with delight. "With Baby Head air freshener, your entire home can smell as fresh as a baby's head." An air freshener, in the shape of an infant's Kewpie doll head filled the screen.

Ozzy walked over to Eaton's cot. He lifted the tarp and sniffed the top of the corpse's head. Eaton's sardonic face was repulsive—but remarkably well preserved.

Ozzy shook his head, "You're not decomposing well at all."

He adjusted the pillow under the corpse's head. "Don't worry, Ben, when we get outta here, I'll bury you some place nice and warm, like Florida—lots of bugs *there*. You'll rot good in Florida." Ozzy pulled the tarp over Eaton's corpse. "Natural decomposition—that's the final luxury, Ben."

~

Days later, Ozzy read a vintage *Haunt of Fear* comic book and periodically glanced up at a World War II documentary on the Military Channel. He dropped the comic when a squadron of B-17s and their fighter escorts came on the screen.

"March 24, 1945. B-17 engines drone in the skies above central Germany," the narrator said, "Red tailed P-51 Mustangs of the 332nd fighter group escort the Flying Fortresses to their target—a tank assembly plant, just outside Berlin. But as the bombers near their target, they spot ominous contrails. A pack of ME 262s goes in for the kill."

"Those Mustangs can handle anything Göering throws at 'em," Ozzy said to the TV.

"I don't think so, Ozzy. The Messerschmitt 262 was a jet, as you well know." Eaton's cadaver sat, shivering, on the folding chair next to Ozzy.

Ozzy leaped out of his recliner.

Eaton's corpse continued, "They could accelerate to 500 miles per hour."

Ozzy peered over the back of the recliner. "You're dead."

"Not nearly dead enough," Ben said.

"Then go back to your fucking cot and try a little harder."

Eaton's corpse started to shiver. "Your rant about freezing down here—it's all true. I'm scared."

"You're sure scarin' the shit outta me, Ben."

"Help me, Ozzy."

Eaton's corpse rose up—stump flailing. He hopped on one leg, fell and zombie crawled toward Ozzy.

Ozzy backed up into the bathroom, slammed the door and leaned against it.

"Help me, Ozzy. Please."

Ozzy whipped around. Eaton's corpse was right behind him.

"You're not real. Go away."

Eaton grabbed Ozzy's hand and blew. It blanched with frost.

"Do you like being cold?" the corpse said.

Ozzy shook his head and rubbed his hand.

"Neither do I. Burn me," said Eaton's corpse.

"I can't do that."

"Burn me. I can't afford the luxury of natural decomposition."

"I can't go outside, not with all those—"

"Do it here. Do it now," Eaton said.

"I'd burn up too."

"Yes, yes you would. Can't you see it would be for the best?"

"But there's a rescue party on the way," Ozzy said.

"And what if the mutants find them before they find us?"

"If we can just hold on for a few—"

"Billion years?" the corpse snarled, "As you so aptly pointed out."

Ozzy covered his face. "You're not real. Leave me alone."

He lowered his hands an inch at a time—Eaton's corpse was gone.

Ozzy burst through the bathroom door, turned on the lights, dashed to Eaton's cot and lifted the tarp. There was Eaton's cadaver—exactly as he left it.

On screen, a P-51 attacked a ME 262, head on. The narrator said, "One of the Tuskegee Airmen, Lieutenant Earl Lane, has a 262 in his sights and fires." The Nazi jet burst into flames.

Ozzy gazed down at Eaton's corpse and said, "You don't know dick about aerial combat."

~

Hours later, Ozzy sat cross-legged on his La-Z-Boy, rattling a box of safety matches and staring vacantly at a red gasoline can on the recliner's footrest. On TV, a televangelist, Reverend Loudermilk, ranted about the end times as he scribbled elaborate diagrams on a clear Lucite marker-board.

Ozzy glanced back at the tarp-covered cot in the corner. "Hey Ben, it's that preacher with the *Flock of Seagulls* hair."

"The science of Satan is an abomination in the eyes of the Lord. Clones, stem cells, evolution—the DNA code," the reverend said, "Ever wonder what DNA stands for?"

"Deoxyribonucleic acid," Ozzy answered with certainty.

Reverend Loudermilk wrote out *his* answer on the marker-board. "The <u>D</u>evil's <u>N</u>ecromantic <u>A</u>lphabet."

Ozzy put down the matches and grabbed the remote.

Zap, Zap.

On TV, the news anchor said, "This just in from Antarctica."

Lorelei stood next to a deep crevasse. Sno-Cat headlights, flashlights, and harsh video camera lights illuminated the EDI rescue expedition. There was considerable activity and shouting as the group gathered around the crevasse. A camera panned down. The twisted wreckage of the shooters' vehicle lay wedged at the apex of the V-shaped chasm.

Lorelei struggled to keep the hood of her parka from blowing back in the wind. "The rescue team has recovered an unidentified body and a cache of automatic weapons from the wreckage of a high-performance snow vehicle, at the bottom of this treacherous crevasse."

The camera zoomed in on a handsome Asian lad as he examined a frozen corpse wearing a white parka with a red wolf patch.

Hey, it's one of the L'ordre whatever the fuck.

On screen, Lorelei continued, "The rescue party's medic, Darnell Noguchi, is attending to the body now."

The camera framed Darnell snapping one of the corpse's frozen arms to its side, then the other. In the background, Brad and Chad winced with every snap, and so did Ozzy.

Whose idea was it to bring those ass-hatters along?

Darnell stuffed the cadaver into a body bag. The shooter's frozen face filled the screen as Darnell zipped the black bag closed.

Lorelei affected a solemn tone for her voice over, "Days without a sunset. Nights without a dawn. There is a rhythm to Antarctica that can only be fully understood by the sterile ice and the long, long dead."

When he realized he was on camera, Darnell made duck lips and killed the moment.

Ozzy laughed. *I love this guy.*

"Hang on, Ben, we can hold out a little longer." Ozzy said to the corpse on the cot.

Ozzy rummaged through a box full of files and papers. Without turning around, he said, "Sayer is gonna kill us if we don't have some kinda report when he gets here."

On TV, a Japanese version of the *Antiques Road Show* was in progress. Appraisers examined Asian art treasures. The white-gloved connoisseurs pawed the fine raku pottery, 19th century woodblock prints, and antique weapons with care.

Ozzy sat upright in his La-Z-Boy, trying to write six months' worth of reports in one sitting.

Okay, okay, I can do this. I'll start with a timeline and just add the details I can remember.

Ozzy scribbled in a legal pad with a pencil stub.

On TV, a Japanese hipster set an action figure down on the appraiser's table. The expert went nuts. Amid the exuberant conversation, in Japanese, Ozzy could clearly understand the words *Edgar Allan Poe*. Ozzy leaned forward in his recliner and set the legal pad on the floor. When he saw an Edgar Allan Poe action figure, he dove for the TV. Ozzy squinted to understand what they were saying, as if that would somehow help him understand Japanese. As the segment ended, the estimated value of the action figures appeared below: *160,000 YEN*.

Ozzy turned to Eaton's corpse, "Shit. I've got that action figure, Ben. How much is 160,000 yen in our money?"

Ozzy ran to the storage shelves, and dumped the contents of a cardboard box on the floor.

I know he's here somewhere.

Ozzy rifled through an odd assortment of action figures and comic books. There were dozens of instant gourmet coffee packets mixed in with the collectibles. Ozzy stuffed the coffee packets in his pocket, and continued rummaging through his action figures. He found Elvis, Leatherface, a Robonatrix figure, Mulder and Scully, then the master of the macabre himself wedged between Buffy and Vampirella. *Yes.*

Where the hell are you? You have to be here.

Ozzy flung figures from the box as he dug deeper. Jules from Pulp Fiction, then Vincent tumbled to the floor.

C'mon, c'mon I know you're in here, somewhere, damn it.

Without looking, Ozzy dug down deep, and fished around the parameter of the cardboard box.

There you are, my ominous bird of yore.

Ozzy raised Poe's plastic raven in triumph, the accessory that made the figure so rare and valuable. He snapped the red eyed bird onto the poet's shoulder. One more search of the treasure box produced Poe's display stand. He scrutinized the action figure from every angle.

No paint loss. Tight limbs. Flawless injection molding. Near mint—all day long.

Ozzy positioned Poe on the recliner armrest, and stepped back to admire its near-mintyness.

"Hey Ben, check it out. Poe's got his raven. I memorized that poem in twelfth grade. Wrote an essay about it, even. Mr. Dolinski gave me an A. He was so cool. Talked like Bela Lugosi. Kinda looked like him, too."

Peevish Prepsters

Frank Sayer surveyed the automatic weapons, salvaged from the wreckage in the crevasse.

Why would anybody need all these submachine guns in Antarctica?

He picked one up like a man who was accustomed to handling firearms.

These are all Uzis. Full auto—and they're loaded, with the bolt open.

One by one, Sayer slid the bolts closed so they couldn't fire.

I don't get it. Some bad shit is going on down here, and I don't want to find out the hard way.

Sayer waved to Roy Cooper, a burly, Kiwi, Sno-Cat driver. "Hey Roy, help me load all thith hardware into our Thno-Cat."

Roy cut Darnell off mid-sentence and hustled over to Sayer. "That bloke is mad as a cut snake. He was giving me a bloody earbashing."

Sayer and Roy each gathered up an armload of weapons and headed for their Sno-Cat.

"What about all those loaded magazines and boxes of nine millimeters?" Roy said.

"They're coming with uth too."

Sayer and Roy headed for their Sno-Cat.

"Guns aren't allowed in Antarctica, you know," Roy said.

"I'll turn them over to the thtation manager when we get back to McMurdo—along with the body. They can thort all thith crazy thit out."

As they unloaded the guns in the rear cargo area of their Sno-Cat, Sayer noticed Brad pacing the ice and mumbling to himself as Chad looked on from inside the cab of his Sno-Cat.

Sayer stormed over to the inept prepsters. "What are you thlackers waiting for? Put that body in the back of your Thno-Cat. C'mon, get movin'."

Chad climbed down from the cab.

They both approached the body bag with great hesitation. They scrutinized the ominous, black bag with the apprehension of nervous used car shoppers.

Brad folded his arms. "I'm not touching that thing."

"Don't tell *me* about it," Chad said glancing at Sayer.

"It's bad luck to ride with a dead guy, Mr. Sayer," Brad said.

"Where the fuck did you hear that?" Sayer said.

"It's common knowledge."

Chad shrugged his shoulders and nodded.

Guys like that can screw up a mission and get everyone killed.

"Okay then. Listen up. Thtow that body-bag in the back of my Thno-Cat, but be quick about it. And when you're done with that, thtay in your cab and thut the fuck up. Got it?"

"Yes sir, My Sayer," Brad said.

They both saluted.

Don't tempt me. In the army, we had a way of dealing with guys like this.

Sayer gave them a dismissive wave and hustled to catch up with Roy. They plodded back to the remaining weapons and Lorelei handling one of the Uzis.

Roy said, "Put that bloody thing down, it's loaded."

Sure hope I closed the bolt on that one. All we need now is a gun crazy journalist to shoot somebody.

Sayer jogged the last few yards to her side.

Lorelei struck a pose with the gun. "Can I shoot it? I did a piece a while back about women in bikinis shooting automatic weapons."

"Did you remember to pack a bikini?" Sayer said.

"Well, no."

"Then, I'm thorry, you can't thoot the machinegun."

Lorelei gave Sayer one of her famous smirk-smiles and handed him the Uzi. He checked the bolt. It was open.

Shit. This bad boy was ready to rumble.

"Remember, the firtht rule of gun thafety: there ith no thuch thing ath an unloaded gun," Sayer yanked out the magazine and showed Lorelei the bullets, "Ethpecially when it ith loaded."

A muffled voice cried inside Sayer's pocket.

What the fuck?

Lorelei stepped back and said, "What the hell was that?"

Sayer rooted around in the pocket of his parka and pulled out his radio handset.

"What is up with you, Brad?" the voice in the handset said.

"That dumbass duo left the radio on in their Thno-Cat," Sayer said.

"Those cute college boys?" Lorelei said.

Sayer almost laughed. "Yeah, Brad and fucking Chad.

"I want to go home."

Sayer raised the handset closer to his ear. "That thoundth like Brad."

"Better not let Mr. Sayer see you cry."

"And that mutht be Chad."

"What's the worst he can do, fire me?" Brad said.

I'll give that little snot something to cry about.

"This is the most exciting thing we've ever done."

"We could freeze to death down here, Chad, if you haven't noticed."

"C'mon, it's totally toasty in the cab."

"Until we fall into one of those ice holes like the dead guy."

Terra passed by Brad and Chad's Sno-Cat trying not to slip on the ice. She smiled and waved. "Hey Chad."

"What's up with you and Terra?" Brad said.

"What do you mean?"

"Her acting all nice and shit after what happened in the lunch room."

"We're good now. I apologized to her last week. You should try it," Chad said.

"She owes *me* an apology." Brad's voice crackled through the handset.

"For what?"

"Hello. She emailed dick pics to my *mother*," Brad said.

Chad's laughter sounded unnaturally loud coming from the device.

"Not funny, Chad."

"Did you get in a lot of trouble?"

"Trouble? It was a fucking nightmare. Name one thing that's worse than that?"

"I'm sure I could think of something, but I can't think of anything off the top of my head."

"That's because there is absolutely nothing worse than sending dick pics to your mother. Nothing. When they make those lists of the top ten things people are afraid of, they need to put sending your mother dick pics at the top of the list. It's way more terrifying than an airplane crash or public speaking."

Roy wandered over with an arm full of Uzis. "Cripes, Frank, even those little bludgers deserve a little privacy."

Sayer shrugged and switched off his handset.

Lorelei grabbed his hand, turned it back on, and said, "Hey, it's just getting good."

"I see what you mean. What did she say?" Chad said.

"So, my mom calls and says, 'Why did you send me all those photographs of your penis, honey?' I didn't know what the fuck to say. Then she says, 'Do you have cancer, sweetie? Why don't you have any hair down there?' The thing is, at first, I didn't know Terra sent them. Then I remembered how she was messing with my phone, and I panicked."

"That's terrible."

"Tell me about it. Luckily, my mom knows next to nothing about computers, so I told her I was hacked by Russians. She seemed to be buying it, but get this, she asked if I was sure they were Russians, because Russian men have much larger penises than the one in the photographs, and they are quite bushy down there."

Sayer turned to Lorelei and said, "Oh, thith thit ith way better than good."

Lorelei smirked in agreement.

"Your mother is pretty crafty," Chad said, laughing.

"Glad you find this so fucking funny."

"You don't get it, do you?"

"Get what?"

"That your mother let your punishment fit the crime. She knew it was your dick. If she was going to have to live with the knowledge her son is a perv, she was going to let you wonder why she knew so much about hirsute Russians with big Ivans."

"Oh my God. She did that?"

"Ask her."

"No, no, no. Are you kidding?"

"Have you been imagining your mother having Russkie sex?"

"Hell yes, I have, and it's driving me crazy. Now, I feel like throwing up every time I even think about sex."

"So, you stopped watching porn?"

"Oh, fuck yeah. No matter what I watch, I picture my mom doing all that fucked up shit with Russian guys."

"Wow. I guess clips of lactating MILFs in bondage would be about the worst."

The sound of the cab door creaking open and violent retching reverberated in Sayer's handset speaker.

Sayer pointed to the prepsters Sno-Cat and said, "Look, that ith Terra waving a Maglight."

Terra's voice was muffled by the windshield. "You all right, Brad? You look sick."

"Go away. This is all your fault," Brad's voice quavered, "This isn't over."

"You have to let it go, buddy," Chad said.

"You're as bad as she is."

The headlights of the Sno-Cat flashed on.

Lorelei raised a tiny digital recorder to her lips and said. "The headlight beam illuminated Terra as she walked away from the surly ice cowboys. A halogen halo encircled the snowbound angel, and her sultry breath filled the crystalline air with magic."

Sayer grabbed Lorelei's wrist. "Wait a minute, you've been recording thith the whole time?"

"Bet your ass, Frank. Like you said, it's better than good. It's NPR good. Peabody good."

Chad said, "Ya know what?"

"No, what?"

"Even in snow pants, Terra has the peachiest ass I think I've ever seen."

"Her ass is evil. Cursed," Brad said.

"C'mon, nothing that beautiful could ever be evil."

"That ass ruined my life."

"I apologized to Terra. She granted me absolution. I can gaze upon her ass with innocent wonder, light of heart and free from guilt."

"You're shitting me, right?"

"Maybe a little."

"How can you joke around like that? Can't you see I'm in agony over this?"

"This whole thing sounds so Greek, bro. You're like Prometheus. He stole fire from the gods and gave it to all mankind. You stole the image of Terra's smokin' hot ass to share with all mankind. You got caught, and now you're doomed to suffer eternal punishment. Is that sick, or what?"

"That's supposed to make me feel better?"

"Fuck no, it's supposed to give you perspective on the tragedy that is your life."

A screech sounded in the near distance.

Lorelei said, "What was that?"

Sayer thought for a second and said, "It'th just the crevasstheth telling uth we need to get the fuck out of here.

Reaper Ripper

Terra gazed out the rear window of Sayer's Sno-Cat at the other two mammoth vehicles as they lumbered across the desolate ice sheet.

Why do I feel so lonely with all those other people around?

Brad and Chad's Sno-Cat, with provisions lashed to the roof, followed close behind. Lorelei and her crew's Sno-Cat, with a satellite dish on top, brought up the rear. Loud music inside Sayer's vehicle drowned out the deafening wail of the wind.

Terra turned her attention to the GPS handset and the topographical map in her lap.

She sat between Sayer and Roy, the Sno-Cat's driver. The hulking Kiwi's gnarly hands gripped the steering wheel at ten and two. They could have been the hands of a plumber or more likely a fighter of some kind. His nose had clearly been broken more than once.

Terra struggled to concentrate as Frank Sayer helped Martha and the Vandellas sing *Heat Wave* with way too much soul for a man his age.

Terra said, "Quick question, Mr. Sayer," and turned the music down.

"Hey, hey, hey, the music ith keeping me warm," Sayer said.

"Do these coordinates look right to you?" Terra said.

"They don't have to look right. They jutht are right. Right Roy?

Roy glanced at the GPS. "Right, Frank," Roy said, "give or take a few inches."

Terra folded up the map, and said, "You sure have a lot of songs, Mr. Sayer."

"Thith ith my hot theme playlitht."

"How many hot songs could there be?" Terra said.

"Exactly eighty-theven."

"*Fever*, Peggy Lee," Roy said.

"Hot theme, but too jazzy," Sayer said.

"*Black Hole Sun*," Roy said.

"Got it."

"*Here Comes the Sun*." Roy said.

"Got it."

"*Burning Down the House*," Terra said.

"Talking Headth. Got it." Sayer grinned.

Roy thought hard. "*Walkin' on Sunshine*."

Sayer winced. "Thit. Need it. Eighty-eight."

"*Ring of Fire*," Terra said.

"That'th country," Sayer said, "Johnny Cath."

"Not the Wall of Voodoo cover," Terra said with a sly grin.

Sayer winced again. "Damn. Eighty-nine."

"Anything this century?" Terra said.

Sayer tracked forward to *Set Fire to the Rain* by Adele.

"I'm impressed," Terra said.

"It's amazing how many songs have a hot theme," Roy said.

"When we get back, I think I'll work on a rain theme play-litht," Sayer said.

"What about magic songs?" Terra said.

"Hell yeth," Sayer said, "*Black Magic Woman, I Put a Thpell on You, Mythtic Eyeth.*"

"*Witchy Woman, Do You believe in Magic,*" Terra said.

Roy raised his hand. "What about songs with a love theme?"

Sayer and Terra glared at Roy like he was insane.

He just doesn't get it.

When Terra reached back into the rear cargo area, to stow her map, she was surprised to see the black body bag. It rested as peacefully as could be expected surrounded by the salvaged automatic weapons and boxes of ammunition.

She tapped her boss on the shoulder as he belted out the chorus to *Summer in the City*. "I hate to bother you, Mr. Sayer, but did you know there was a body in the back?"

"Yeah. I told thoth thlackerth they could put it there."

"Why did you even bring them with us?"

"If it wath up to me, I would have fired them long ago."

"You're the boss."

"Ath long ath I don't ruffle any of the donor'th featherth. Ever hear of the Caldwell Fund?"

"Yeah, it's one of those shady hedge funds."

"What ith Chad'th latht name?"

"Caldwell."

"The Caldwell family ith our number one donor."

"It's Brad I can't stand."

"Hith family ith rich, but they're not wealthy. They don't give uth a dime. They're card-carrying climate change denierth."

"So, fire him."

"Unfortunately, they come as a pair. The ruleth of entitlement apply to friendth, and even friendth of friendth."

Terra pointed to the body bag. "Did you see that?"

A bulbous shape moved from one end of the bag to the other.

"What?"

"I saw something move in there—inside the bag."

"I don't thee anything."

Roy chimed in, "It's probably gas escaping from the corpse as it heats up."

"Gross," Terra said.

Roy laughed. "Ever smelled a reaper ripper, cuz?"

Terra winced. "Noooo."

Sayer said, "And I thuppose you have?"

"Oh, sure, mate. Once you smell a reaper ripper, you'll never forget it. They smell like a cross between rotten eggs and a holiday gift basket."

Nausea and morbid curiosity competed for Terra's reaction to what she was hearing. Morbid curiosity won out.

"So, where did you smell these reaper rippers?" Terra said, as she turned the music off.

"Don't pay any attention to him, Terra. He'th just yanking your chain."

"Let him finish," Terra said.

"Well, miss, I was a wharfie on the docks up in Auckland. Every now and then, there'd be a container that would stank up the yard—all the way downtown."

"What wath inthide?"

"Dead things, boss. All manner of dead things."

"You're going to give Terra bad dreamth. Better leave it at that."

"No. no, I need to know—now," Terra said.

"Are you sure? There are some stories you can't unhear, once they've been told—no matter how hard you try," Roy closed his eyes and shuddered, "And you can't never unsmell a reaper ripper—never."

Terra rubbed her sweaty hands on her snow pants and said, "Okay, Roy I'm ready. What was the worst one?"

Roy drummed his fingers on the steering wheel, and shook his head. "Can't tell you about the worst one. It's too sad, and I'll get all choked up," He smiled and said, "But I'll tell you all about the weirdest one."

Terra studied Roy's face as he scanned the ice ahead for crevasses. He didn't strike her as a teller of tall tales. She sensed he was a man who traded imagination for street smarts a long time ago.

Roy continued, "It was December of '09. It's summer for us in New Zealand, so it was hot as hell. We unloaded a big shipment of containers from Jakarta, mainly tires and rare wood. It wasn't unusual to get shipments from Indonesia. They're a major trading partner. Anyway, most of the containers were in pretty good shape, fresh paint and all. But there was this one that just looked like trouble. It was dented and rusted through in places. After a few days on the yard, the stank raised suspicion."

Terra studied Roy's face. He scrunched his fighter's nose like he could still smell it now.

"Did you break it open and look inside," Terra said.

Roy nodded, then shook his head like he wished the answer was no. "We called the coppers and they cut the lock.

My Maori mate, Rongo, opened the door. Bloody hell. What we saw was like something out of a horror movie, or one of those gory stories. This guy was strapped into a car seat that had been welded to the floor of the container. He'd been dead for a few days. His body was all bloated up, to the point where his clothes were the only thing keeping him from just blowing the fuck up, pardon my French. Here's where it gets weird."

Terra glance over at Sayer. "You okay Mr. Sayer? You don't look so good."

"Yeah, yeah, I'm fine," Sayer said, "I jutht know thith thtory will not end well."

"So, what happened to him?" Terra said.

Roy shivered as he continued. "The bloke was covered with all these little lizards. They had eaten his face and hands—right down to the bone. Not a drop of blood anywhere, though. But get this, the guy had all these comforts in that container, a little chemical toilet, a camping stove, LED lights. He even had one of those pricey laptops—and a cell. The coppers argued about who was going in there to unstrap Mr. Skullface's seatbelt. Guess what? This lady copper was the only one who would go inside. In retrospect, they should have waited for the coroner. What happened next was bloody disgusting. I really shouldn't go on."

Terra clutched Roy's massive forearm. "Oh no. No, no, no—I want to hear the rest of the darn story."

"I'm thurprised you want to hear thomething tho dithurbing."

"Why? Because I'm a girl?"

"I didn't thay that."

"You didn't have to. You're the one who looks disturbed."

"Thute yourthelf."

"Did they ever find out who the guy in the container was?" Terra said.

"Yeah. It was in all the Kiwi papers. He was this Yank college student. I forget his name. The kid had this swiftie business going to pay his tuition at some fancy school. The bludger smuggled endangered species, from all over the world, and sold them for pets to rich blokes. All those little lizards, they were baby Komodo Dragons. Very rare—and very nasty. There were dozens of them. The aquarium he was transporting them in musta broke. Those shipping containers really get jostled around. That's why the wanker rigged up the car seat. The tosser musta got bit. Komodo Dragons aren't poisonous, but their saliva is so festy with bacteria, it's deadly. In the wild, they can take down a full-grown water buffalo. All they have to do is get one good bite in. They'll track that water buffalo, sometimes for days, until it's too sick to run, then dinner is served. That's what happened to the kid. The coroner said he died of blood poisoning from a bad infection."

"Septicemia," Terra said.

"Right. Musta been a slow, painful death. Hope he died before the little buggers ate his face."

Sayer said, "Can we talk about thomething a little more cheerful?"

Roy drew a deep breath and exhaled his words, "Sure thing, mate. Seen any good cable shows, lately? Last week I binged two whole seasons of—"

Terra shook Roy's arm. "Forget about that. What happened to the police woman?

"Well, like I was saying, what happened next was bloody disgusting. The lady copper walked right into that container and started fiddling with the dead guy's seat belt. Then blammo, the belt flies off. At this point, I have to explain that the seat belt was holding in all that trapped gas—pent-up death gas— under pressure."

Roy leaned closer to Terra, gazed into her eyes like he was looking for something and whispered, "What I saw next was beyond anything on one of those forensic TV shows."

I watch them all, so bring it on big guy.

Roy turned his attention to the ice ahead and continued. "The force of all that foul gas shooting out of the corpse's arsehole, actually lifted the bloated cadaver up and off the car seat. The lady copper backed up, but not before the hideous thing knocked her on her arse—and landed right on top of her. Did she lose her shit? No, no she did not. She rolled the bloated gas-bag over onto its stomach, and hopped up with a cheesy grin like it was nothin'. But then she started batting at her head. Turns out, it was one of those damn lizards. A baby Komodo was all tangled up in her hair."

Terra shuddered. "Did she—"

Roy laughed. "Did she lose her shit? Yes, yes she did. Wish I thought to get my phone out and film the dance she did, but I was, like, in the moment, if you know what I mean. She took hold of the miniature monster, but its tiny claws were really tangled in her hair, so she just yanked the little bastard—hair and all. She looked at it for a second, as it snapped and squirmed in her hand. Then she just tossed it back in the shipping container. Didn't kill it or anything. Tiny trickles of blood ran down her forehead where the vicious creature bit her scalp. We just stood there watching all this. Meanwhile, the reaper rippers kept on comin'. Ever had one of those whoopee cushions when you were a kid? It sounded like that, except wetter, much wetter. That nasty arse just kept farting—on, on and on, and on. And the smell—bloody hell—the smell. Let me tell you something, people say shit like, I saw this or that movie and it was really scary, or there was a big spider in the bathtub. I was terrified, or so and so's new book is a masterpiece of horror. None of that means shit. I'll tell you what horror is. Horror is that smell. The acrid odor of death gas escaping from a rotting corpse's arsehole. I'm no expert on brain science, but I know this—there are receptors, or whatever, in our brains that know that stench. You smell that stank once, just one time, and you will have smelled every corpse littered battlefield, every body ever trapped in earthquake rubble, every mass grave and plague pit. Throughout history, no matter what time and place—horror smells the same."

The Sno-Cat cab fell silent. Terra started to say something to her boss, but when she saw him sitting there with his eyes closed, she sensed he was somewhere far away.

I bet Mr. Sayer has a gory story or two to tell, but he's not talking.

Terra looked over at Roy. His hands shook, even though he clinched the steering wheel tight. He stared out the windshield at something far beyond the throw of the searchlight beam.

Terra's Tito

Hours later, Terra provided a second set of eyes for possible danger as Sayer's Sno-Cat rumbled across the treacherous ice-sheet.

Inside the cab, Foreigner's *Hot Blooded* drowned out the blizzard's roar. Terra couldn't get Roy's story out of her head. It unlocked long forgotten doors in the forbidden corridors of her mind.

Doors have locks for a reason. They keep bad things out, but more importantly, they lock even worse things in—like morbid fascinations, unwholesome desires, irrational fears, all the things good girls are taught to hide.

Terra closed her eyes.

She ran to the lime green door at the end of the corridor and pushed it open. Inside was an open coffin. Swaddled in pleated satin lay her Tito. Her grandfather died when she was six. She had never seen a dead person before, or after, for that matter—until today. Her grandfather didn't look dead. In fact, he looked better than ever.

Why is everybody crying? Tito is just sleeping.

Terra begged her mother to help Tito out of the box.

Can't you see he's sleeping. Wake him up. Let's go home.

The more Terra argued with her mother, the harder her mother cried.

Tito is going to miss his wrestling. He said I could stay up late and watch it with him. The ginger ale you bought him is in the refrigerator.

Terra's father tried to calm her down, but it just made her madder. He told her Tito was in heaven now, and it was time to say goodbye.

If Tito is so dead, why is he wearing his glasses? Dead people don't need glasses? Why is he smiling? This is all a big mistake. Everybody stop crying and let's go home.

Terra ran to Tito's coffin and rested her tiny hands on his. His big hands were as cold as the plastic rosary they so reverently clutched. It would have been so much easier to accept her grandfather's death if there was even a whiff of that reaper ripper smell Roy talked about. Tito smelled like cleaning fluid and too many different kinds of flowers. Terra ran from Tito's room and slammed the lime green door.

A familiar voice called her name, "Terra, Terra, rithe and thine." Frank Sayer shook her shoulder, "Have you been crying?"

Terra wiped tears from her eyes, and said, "I'm okay. Bad dream, that's all."

Sayer leaned over Terra and glared at Roy. "Look what you did. You gave Terra nightmareth with your gory thtory."

Roy pushed Sayer away. "Sorry, Terra. I never meant to—"

"No, no, no, Roy," Terra said, "It's all on me."

And this place. It keeps nightmares and gory stories on ice. Fresh frozen. Just waiting for the thaw.

Black Bag

Terra sat with her chin on her knees, arms wrapped tight around her shins.

I always wanted to go on an adventure somewhere dangerous but not a place like this. It's so dark. Darker than dark. Perpetual midnight. I hope Ozzy is all right.

Sayer pointed out the window. "Hey, whath that?"

"What?" Roy slowed down.

Terra stretched her legs out straight and peered out the windshield.

Sayer turned down the music. Motley Crue's *Red Hot* squeaked on in the background.

"Up ahead. On your left." Sayer flipped on the full bank of searchlights.

"Bloody hell." Roy brought the Sno-Cat to a full stop.

Colonel Pomeroy's abandoned chopper stood motionless in the harsh light. The doors gaped open. The surrounding snow glistened red like a thousand rubies—frozen blood.

"Flag the coordinateth of that helicopter," Sayer said to Terra, "We'll check it out later."

Terra reached in the back to mark their location on her map.

A bulbous shape undulated inside the body bag. Terra started to say something, when a bloody beak ripped through the body bag, and she screamed instead.

Sayer and Roy whipped around.

A mutant penguin peered through the rip in the body bag. Its blazing, red eyes darted back and forth.

The little monster *screeched*, lunged at Roy and snipped off his right ear.

Roy bellowed and grabbed his gushing ear hole.

The penguin just glared at them from atop the body bag.

"Oh shit," Terra said.

The Sno-Cat skidded to a stop.

The mutant clutched Roy's ear in its beak.

"If we get that ear, Darnell can put it back on." Sayer said.

Terra peeked up from behind her seat. "Drop the nice man's ear Mr. Penguin. C'mon pretty birdie."

"Fuck that," Roy said and climbed over the seat.

The penguin tossed his head back and Roy's ear disappeared into its gullet.

"Gimme back my ear!" Roy crawled over his seat and lunged.

The bird snapped, and snipped off his other ear. The penguin gulped it down whole.

Roy scooted backward, spread-eagle, holding both gaping ear holes.

The snapping little monster stared at his crotch.

Roy slammed his knees together.

The creature screeched and jumped on Roy's chest.

Terra swatted the bird with a snowshoe.

Sayer grabbed an Uzi from the back and leveled it at the creature.

Terra looked out the rear window and watched members of their rescue party pile out of their Sno-Cats to see what was going on.

Flashlight beams outside transformed the windows inside the cab into bloody stained glass.

Brad opened the rear cargo doors. "Hey, what's going on in—"

Terra waved him away, "Get back!"

The mutant penguin dove through the open door and stabbed Brad's abdomen.

The impact pushed Brad back and he hit the ice belly up. Flippers and quivering viscera protruded from the front of his blood-soaked parka.

Chad rushed over to him. "Brad."

Sayer bounded out of the cab and shoved Chad out of the way.

Terra joined Chad to see if she could help Brad, but reeled back as Brad's body heaved up and down in an increasingly violent series of spasmodic jerks.

I will not scream. I will not scream. I will not scream.

Sayer rolled the body over. The devil bird's head jutted out of Brad's back.

Sayer blew it off with a single *brup* from his Uzi.

The news crew scattered.

Sayer yanked the mutant out of Brad's abdomen by the flippers.

Lorelei loomed over the body like a statue.

Sayer unfolded his utility knife and slashed open the creature's bloated stomach.

Blood sprayed across Lorelei's unflinching face.

Terra watched, in disbelief, as Sayer fished out one of Roy's ears—then the other.

Lorelei seemed to devour the insane scene with hungry eyes.

Sayer handed her the bloody ears. "Hang on to them till I come back with Darnell. He can put them back on."

Lorelei examined the ears with detached curiosity, and said, "Shouldn't we put these on ice?"

Precious Poe

Back in the Pit, Ozzy sipped instant espresso as he positioned his Edgar Allan Poe action figure on the armrest of the recliner. After his third cup, the combination of caffeine, sugar, and starvation loosened Ozzy's already feeble grip on reality. "Hey, Ben, you up for a poetry recital?"

The audience waited with injection-molded enthusiasm on the seat cushion. Jules and Vincent from Pulp Fiction, Robonatrix, Leatherface, Elvis, Mulder and Scully and their alien had front row seats. Non-VIP action figures had to settle for the cheap seats on the floor.

Ozzy recited *The Raven* from behind the recliner in a convincing southern accent, "Once upon a midnight dreary, while I pondered, weak and weary, over many a quaint and curious volume of forgotten lore. While I nodded, nearly napping, suddenly there came a tapping, as of someone gently rapping, rapping at my chamber door. 'Tis some visitor,' I muttered, tapping at my chamber door. Only this, and nothing more.'"

The X Files Alien skulked toward the armrest stage and interrupted the reading. "Rengee otrum, puvigete woot woot maxufurtum songoreti baaworto cax rax poonee."

Poe stopped reciting, and turned to Fox Mulder. "What did your odd-looking companion say, sir?"

"Please don't take offense, Mr. Poe, but he said rhyming poetry in trochaic octameter is passé, and that free verse is more acceptable to contemporary sensibilities. You must forgive him, he's not of this world, and unaware you wrote your poem over one hundred and fifty years ago."

Elvis said, "I hate horror poetry, rhymin' or not. Lose the

weirdo, and I'll sing *It's Now or Never*. Let's liven up this clam bake."

Dana Scully said, "I would respectfully suggest, Mr. Presley, that *The Raven* isn't actually a horror poem. Sure, it's atmospheric and melancholy, but it's really more of a romantic poem. You know, like a sad love song."

Mulder said, "Depending on a person's state of mind, a bird tapping at a door and the rustling of a curtain could be frightening. Not Peacock Family frightening, but pretty damn disturbing. Given the right lighting and fog effects even my green friend here could be terrifying."

The alien leaped forward. "Voritti, Voritti non."

Leatherface brandished his chainsaw above his head, "Brum-brum-brum-brrrrrrrrrrrrr. "

The alien made a break for it across the recliner's cushion. "Be be batag kago yon. Be be batag kago yon."

Leatherface took off after the alien with his chainsaw, and dispatched the screaming extraterrestrial without mercy.

Mulder said, "Okay, now that's scary."

Jules climbed to the armrest opposite the stage, a briefcase in one hand, a gun in the other. He raised his nickel plated .45 and said, "Yo, all y'all don't know shit about narrative poetry," he gestured to Poe using his .45 as a pointer, "You see my southern gentleman over here? Well, he's one of the rhyminest motherfuckers who ever lived. Dig this, 'Though thy crest be shorn and shaven, thou art sure no craven, Ghastly grim and ancient raven wandering from the Nightly shore. Tell me what thy lordly name is on the Night's Plutonian shore! Quoth the Raven, Nevermore.' Now, that's some deep shit. Shallow end of the pool motherfuckers like you could drown just listenin' to deep shit like that. I'm going to say this one time and one time only. If you do not shut the fuck up, I will not hesitate to pop a cap in all yo whiny ass asses. Let-the-man-finish-his-motherfucking-poem."

Poe gave Jules a knowing nod, "I thank you, sir. You are too kind. Your words are both generous, and much appreciated."

Poe continued his poem, uninterrupted. He delivered the

last stanza with haunting urgency, "And the Raven, never flitting, still is sitting, still is sitting, On the pallid bust of Pallas just above my chamber door; And his eyes have all the seeming of a demon's that is dreaming, And the lamplight o'er him streaming throws his shadow on the floor; And my soul from out that shadow that lies floating on the floor, Shall be lifted—nevermore!"

Ozzy rushed the Robonatrix action figure to the armrest stage. He had her sashay up to Poe. "Oh Edgar," said Ozzy in a hoarse falsetto, "You're my favorite dark poet."

The Robonatrix wrapped her articulated arms around Poe's neck, and her legs around his waist. She rode the bewildered poet like a pole dancer and said, "Did your little Annabel Lee do ya like this, Eddy baby?"

Poe stumbled in circles, trying to keep from losing his balance and falling off the armrest. "No, madam, I can assure you she certainly did not. Annabel was a fragile flower and she would never do, do—that—oh, oh that. For the love of all the seraphim in the firmament, please continue doing *that*."

Elvis burst upon the scene. "Hey man, that's way too much woman for a scrawny weirdo like you." He turned to the Robonatrix, and said, "C'mon momma, I'm taking you home with me."

Robonatrix said, "Get lost."

"I'll buy ya a pink Cadillac, darlin'."

"Like the one you bought Barbie, you Elvis impersonating, plastic, piece of shit?"

Poe popped Elvis in the nose, and he tumbled onto the cushion. The king leaped up and struck a karate pose.

Ozzy brought Jules and Vincent into the action. Jules said, "Yo, Poe. We got this shit." They raised their .45s and fired.

Plastic Elvis took a dozen shots, before tumbling to the floor.

Jules turned to Fox Mulder, pointed to Poe and Robonatrix and said, "Ya know what that is?"

Mulder said, "So, I can stop shutting the fuck up now, without getting shot?"

Jules said, "Yeah, yeah."

"What do you think it is?"

"Poetry in motherfucking motion."

The Robonatrix hammered Poe harder. "C'mon baby, say something dark and poetic."

"Uh—flowers wilt in my true love's tomb."

"That's it. I'm almost there. Gimme just a little more."

"Cold like her, in that granite womb."

"Oh, God, oh, God, oh, God, oh God."

"Oweeshit! Stop squeezin' so hard," Poe said.

"What, never banged a multi-orgasmic, robotic dominatrix before?"

"*Oweeshit—oweeshit—oweeshit!*" Poe thrashed to break free of Robonatrix's merciless grip.

"This just in, a live satellite report from Lorelei Teller in Antarctica," the news anchor said. Ozzy looked up at the TV screen and dropped his love locked action figures. On screen, camera lights tunneled through the darkness, illuminating the charred debris of the devastated science station. Shaky digital video focused on the yawning entrance to the stairwell.

In a panic, Ozzy stashed his action figures under Eaton's cot as the rescue party descended the icy steps.

When they reached the landing, the camera panned the shooter's frozen carcass and stopped on Terra. She covered her eyes, "We didn't get here in time!"

When Ozzy heard Terra's voice, he dashed to the television and touched the screen.

Lorelei's cameraman zoomed in on the corpse's hideous face. Even though the eye sockets had been pecked clean, the hollow voids pleaded to be released from the panic and the pain. The cold had preserved the shooter's gaping mouth, frozen in a silent scream.

"Which one is it?" Lorelei said, off screen.

The camera pulled back to a medium shot of Sayer, Darnell, and Terra.

"Too thin to be Pratt. It hath to be Dr. Eaton," Sayer said.

"This dude's, like, ripped to shit," Darnell said.

Terra grabbed Sayer's arm. "Do you think *Ozzy* is still alive?"

"Only one way to find out." Sayer sidestepped the corpse and tried to open the door. It was locked. He pounded hard, "Pratt, you in there?"

Ozzy said from the other side of the door, "Oh shit. Yeah, yeah, yeah. Be there in a second."

He dropped Poe and Robonatrix in front of the television, stumbled to the door and unlocked the bolt. The door flew open.

In a heartbeat, the room filled with people.

Ozzy shielded his eyes from the glaring camera lights. He looked at the television and saw himself shielding his eyes—repeating to infinity. Ozzy's knees weakened. He wobbled. His eyelids fluttered. Silver spots sparkled in the spinning room. His field of vision dimmed to black.

After a few moments, little fireflies of light flitted around in the darkness, until a circle of faces came into focus: Frank Sayer, Terra Perez, Lorelei Teller and Darnell Noguchi—all looking down at him.

"Give him thome room," Sayer said.

Ozzy grabbed the front of Darnell's parka and pulled him down. "How much is 160,000 yen?"

Darnell looked confused.

"How much is 160,000 yen in dollars? You're Japanese, right?"

"Dude, I was born in Van Nuys," Darnell said.

Darnell lifted Ozzy up and helped him to his cot.

"Check him out," Sayer said to Darnell.

Darnell held his nose as he took Ozzy's pulse. "He's cool, but like, if BO was toxic, we'd all be dead."

Sayer nodded in agreement as he fanned the air. "Everybody out." He turned to Terra, "Exthept you. You can freshen your boyfriend up."

"But—"

"Jutht do it."

Sayer herded the others out and slammed the door behind him.

Terra Time

Terra scanned the room and saw Poe and the Robonatrix on the floor. Ozzy sprang from his cot and scooted in front of the television. He kicked the lewd action figures aside and grabbed the remote.

What was that all about?

"How 'bout some music?" he said.

"That would be great."

Zap, zap, zap.

Ozzy found a music video channel.

Terra was confused. She had a million questions for Ozzy, but he was different. He seemed disoriented—detached.

Ozzy doesn't look the same. Something really bad has happened here, but I'm not going to start asking a bunch of questions. He'll tell me in his own time. What he needs now is some kind attention and a thorough cleaning.

Terra reached out and took both of Ozzy's hands in hers. She squeezed hard, "I missed you, ya know."

Ozzy looked away, but Terra could see his eyes were tearing up. "I missed you, too."

Ozzy took a deep breath, "So, how are things back at EDI?"

"Oh, fine."

"What's up with Sayer?" Ozzy said, "He talks like Thylvethter the Cat."

Terra laughed. "He stabbed his tongue with a plastic fork, a couple of weeks ago. It needed tons of stitches."

"Ouch."

Terra spotted a teapot on the hotplate and switched it on. She surveyed the room. "Any soap, a washcloth?"

"There's some soap in the bathroom. No washcloths."

Terra picked up a large sponge from a plastic bucket. "This'll have to do."

"You wouldn't happen to have any food on you?"

Terra pulled three energy bars from her pocket. "Would you like Strawberry Yogurt, Almond Crunch, or Honey Peanut?"

"I'd like 'em *all*."

Terra handed him the bars. Ozzy stared at them for a moment, ripped off the wrappers, and stuffed them all in his mouth at once.

Terra lugged the bucket to the bathroom and filled it half full with water. When the kettle whistled, she added boiling water and set it down while she took off her parka. Her low-cut sweatshirt hung down over one bare shoulder. She wiggled out of her bulky snow pants, revealing skin-tight Levis underneath.

Terra rolled up her sleeves like she was going to wash her car on a sunny, Saturday afternoon and carried the bucket over to Ozzy.

He chomped away at the energy bars as she unzipped his gamy parka. The alpha penguin's skull popped out.

Terra recoiled.

"It's a trophy head, like a talisman," Ozzy said, with his mouth full.

Terra ran her finger down the penguin's massive beak.

This penguin was way bigger that the one that attacked us. How many of these creatures are out there?

She pulled the zipper down further and peeled back his filthy parka. Ozzy's chest was a broad expanse of well-defined muscle. His stomach was as cut as an Abercrombie & Fitch model. He looked down at his newfound muscles in disbelief.

Ozzy took off his boots and snow pants and headed for the trash grinder. He opened the door to the chute and stuffed his parka and snow pants inside. "This might help clear the air."

Terra eyeballed him as she removed her heavy snow boots. She could tell he knew she was watching him by the way he struck a pose as he switched on the grinder.

Terra surveyed Ozzy's brawny physique as he sauntered back to her.

He stood naked, in the center of the room and smiled.

She gazed down at the steaming water, then up at Ozzy. She squeezed the sponge fretfully and said, "I can't believe you're you. You're so, so—"

"Cold?"

"Oh, sorry. Let's get you cleaned up."

Terra scrubbed his strong shoulders. Hot, soapy water cascaded down his rippling back and tumbled over his muscular butt. The sparkling suds fogged the air with fragrant steam. Now, the room smelled clean—day spa clean—prom date clean. Ozzy swung around and raised his arms. Terra scrubbed his chest and stomach in slow, sensuous circles—lower and lower until the sponge hit something. Terra's eyes widened when she felt the magnitude of the obstruction.

Ozzy looked over his shoulder at Terra.

Their eyes locked.

Terra wanted to look away, but couldn't. She grabbed Ozzy's hard-on. A shy smile spread across her face.

Ozzy just grinned.

She thought about letting go, but squeezed tighter instead—the way she'd squeeze the steering wheel of her Prius if she ever drove off a cliff.

With her free hand, Terra unbuttoned her Levis and let them drop to the floor. She wriggled out of her practical panties and flung them across the room with one sure ninja kick.

Ozzy looked down and started to laugh.

Terra scowled, "What?"

She followed his gaze down to her crotch and burst out laughing, too. Steamy wisps of vapor rose from the wet heat between her legs.

Ozzy reached down, cradled Terra's ass and boosted her to his chest. As she rose, Terra never felt so spread open. She had never felt such an eager emptiness or as desperate a need to have it filled.

Terra hiked up the front of her sweatshirt and pressed her soft breasts against his hard chest.

I feel so close to Ozzy. Is this just my body demanding satisfaction for one of its countless cravings, or is it something more?

She could sort all that out later. For the moment, all she wanted was Ozzy inside her, and she wanted him inside her now.

They shared many things before he left for Antarctica: conversations until dawn about their grandest hopes and darkest fears, their favorite movies, music and books—but never a bed.

Ozzy's heart pounded in a syncopated rhythm with her own. His cock throbbed in her hand as she rubbed the swollen tip on her clit.

Madison Kang. Haven't thought about Madison since we were roommates in college. She rented that silly vampire porn movie Ejacula. *We laughed and squealed at the size of the count's veiny impaler as we chomped Cheetos and guzzled Red Bull. Yikes, Ozzy's cock is even bigger than the count's.*

Terra wasn't laughing as she maneuvered Ozzy's angry knob into position. Her sweet cream flowed over her fingers and down his rigid shaft—like melted gelato dripping down a huge sugar cone.

See that? My cunt knows what to do. You don't scare me. Yeah, yeah, you think you're big, but you're not baby-head big. No worries. My cunt knows what to do with you, mister.

Terra pushed down as Ozzy thrusted up, but her vulva was not open for business.

Oh shit. Okay, okay, okay. I take it back. You are big, okay? Whoa fuck. Fuck. fuck. fuck. Easy, now.

Terra panted like she did in her Kundalini Yoga class.

C'mon, breath of fire, don't fail me now. If there's such a thing as a cunt chakra, now's the time to open up and let the serpent rise.

Terra relaxed enough for Ozzy's cock to enter. It disappeared inside her an inch or two at a time. When it hit bottom, with dick to spare, Terra grunted from the brutish pressure.

Did I just grunt like a slavering sow? I never grunt. I'm a sensuous sigher—a girlish gasper.

Ozzy lifted Terra's lithe body up with ease, slammed her hips down and grunted like he took a sucker punch to the gut.

Aha—we're even now. I get it. This is grunty sex. I can do grunty.

Terra dug her fingernails into Ozzy's bulging, trapezius muscles, tossed her head back and rode him like a carousel beast in a dark carnival. Up and down, faster and faster, until the pain inflicted by the monster she created gave way to a slippery bliss she had never experienced before.

Terra wondered who let in the religious fanatic who kept yelling, "Oh God, oh God, oh God," as an old Nine Inch Nails video played on the TV—until she realized the ardent exhortations were her own.

Terra's feverish cravings transported her to a state of hazy delirium. The musky scent of sweet tobacco and spiced rum infused the icy air with lewd illusions. The cramped room dissolved into the cabin of a glowing amber galleon. Terra's deep, rhythmic breaths conspired with her pounding heart to set her adrift on a roiling sea of dangerous imaginings. And then there were pirates—a band of bawdy pirates. They crowded around Terra and Ozzy, gulped rum and masturbated as they leered at her splayed ass with hungry eyes.

Avert your gaze, you mutinous brutes. Can't you see a proper lady is being properly fucked by a proper gentleman?

The vulgar buccaneers just laughed as they spurted liquid pearls all over her quivering flesh.

That's when a rogue swell washed Terra overboard. She bobbed easily on the warm, rolling waves, but the undertow was strong, and she slipped silently beneath the surface. She tried to resist, but it only made the downward pull more intense. Terra surrendered to the tidal surge and plunged deeper into her trembling trance. A languid weakness engulfed her limbs. Swirling currents flowed across her clit. A tingling warmth washed up and back between her stomach and her crotch. Everything went red, and Terra dissolved into the convulsive nothingness of her climax.

Orgasmically Ozzy

Ozzy struggled to keep his balance as Terra shuddered in his arms. As often as he had imagined making love to her, he was overwhelmed by the profound connection he felt with Terra now. Her whole body stiffened, then went completely limp. She drew a deep breath and thrust her hips a few more times—the way a car engine sometimes keeps sputtering after the ignition has been turned off. Ozzy held Terra tighter and wished he could stop time.

The sweat on their glistening skin merged into a single steamy mist. As it rose and swirled in the cold, dry air, it wisped away a lifetime of countless spoken blows. Ozzy had endured the pain of fat shaming long before there was a name for it. He sighed as the cruel little puffs of pain floated toward the ceiling and vanished forever. A metamorphosis had taken place. The man Terra released from that crusty, Gore-Tex cocoon would never have to laugh again when someone called him Fatty Pratty, Oz Lardassian or Boba Fett. He'd never again have to hear his mother tell her American friends that in Nigeria a big man is a successful man.

Ozzy wanted to make the moment last forever. He remained motionless in hopes of delaying the colossal explosion of liquid bliss that had been years in the making. He took a deep breath and regained control over his primal urge to come and be done.

This is working, I got this, I got this.

Then he felt something he hadn't noticed when he was thrusting so hard and fast. Terra's vagina was squeezing his cock in a firm, rippling grip. She wasn't doing it consciously.

It was as if all of nature was greedy for his semen and Terra was an innocent accomplice. He almost let it all go but bit his lip and stole a few more moments from the tyranny of primate evolution.

I'll come at a time of my choosing. I'm no caveman, or some horny monkey in a primeval forest. I'm a man of science, for fuck's sake.

Ozzy gritted his teeth and committed the majority of his 178 IQ points to solving the problem.

How would Richard Feynman break this down? Fluid dynamics. This is definitely a fluid dynamics problem. If I can just calculate the properties of seminal fluid, its flow velocity, pressure, density, and temperature, I can be the boss of this. Okay, okay, I'm pretty sure cum is a non-Newtonian fluid, like emulsions and slurries. They're viscoelastic, thick and sticky like polymers, honey, and, and, lubricants. Terra has the lubricant thing covered—big time. My balls are wet and nasty. Don't think about that. Forget about it. Think about Newton's second law: An accelerating parcel of fluid is subject to inertial effects. Yeah, baby, I got an accelerating parcel of hot, viscous, fluid for you—but not now. No, no, not now. Hear that Mother Nature? You may have Charlie Darwin in your corner, but, Sir Isaac, fucking, Newton has my back, and I'll come when I say. And I say not yet. Now, all I need is Bernoulli's equation to calculate the potential flow. Let's see, the velocity field can be expressed as the gradient of— Shit, oh shit.

Terra's contractions quickened. She reached back and squeezed Ozzy's slippery balls—and that was that.

He bellowed *"gravity"* as he came. His abs and butt clinched in release and agony. Ozzy hadn't factored in the effect of gravity on the vertical velocity of all that seminal fluid. He came slow and hard—and kept on coming. He pulled Terra's hips down and held her tighter. One, two, three massive spurts erupted inside her. He wondered if she could feel the squirt. He looked into her eyes and got the answer.

She gazed back at him with longing and surprise. Her eyes

widened as the throbbing tip of his cock pressed hard against the tiny opening of her cervix, and pumped one last molten load deep inside her.

Ozzy's legs wobbled from muscle fatigue, and the violence of his orgasm. He teetered forward and back to maintain his balance as Terra shifted her weight and rested her head on his shoulder. He was ready to put her down, but she seemed quite content to remain aloft, tethered to his cock.

The heavy steel door swung open. A frigid blast of wind and snow rushed into the living quarters, and so did Sayer and Lorelei.

Terra whipped her head around and screamed.

Ozzy flashed a sheepish grin, hoping the rest of him would become invisible like the Cheshire Cat.

Sayer winced and looked away, "Jeeth loueeth, Terra."

The newswoman nodded as her trademark smirk widened into an actual smile.

Terra pulled the back of her sweatshirt down to cover her ass. She wriggled and squirmed to dismount Ozzy, but she was still hitched securely in place. His cock was still as hard as a table leg as he hoisted Terra the ten inches necessary to disengage.

When he set her down, she scanned the room like a cornered animal.

Ozzy tried to cover his junk with both hands and said, "You could have knocked, Frank."

"Oh, tho, tho, thorry, Pratt. I didn't notice the do not dithturb thign on the door."

Ozzy's heart swelled as Terra snatched up her far-flung panties and faded Levis, queefing madly and trailing steaming spunk behind her.

I love that girl, and I will love her until the end of fucking time.

Terra darted into the bathroom and slammed the door.

Lorelei emitted a lewd growling sound. He felt an odd sense of pride and shame as she licked every square inch of his naked body with her ravenous eyes.

Sayer scowled at Lorelei, "I think you've theen enough," and tossed Ozzy some fresh survival clothes.

As Ozzy pulled a snug thermal shirt over his broad shoulders, Sayer said. "You were morbidly obethe the last time I thaw you."

Ozzy smiled. "What can I say, Frank? It's remarkable what a sensible diet and vigorous exercise can do."

The bathroom door squeaked open. Terra peeked out. Her face was sunburn red. She forced a smile and waved with four fingers, "Hi, guys."

Lorelei ogled Ozzy like a wealthy bidder inspecting a featured lot at a high-end auction.

"You were fat?" Lorelei leered at Ozzy as he wiggled into his snow pants.

"Over 300 pounds."

Terra hustled over to Ozzy and tossed back her hair like nothing had happened.

Lorelei squeezed between them and said, "When we get back, I'd like to do a profile on you, Dr. Pratt. Maybe over dinner. Drinks perhaps?" She traced the contour of his angular jaw with her index finger.

"Pick on somebody your own age," Terra said.

Lorelei smirked at Sayer, "Tell your PR Barbie she'd better play nice if she ever wants to get another sound bite out of me."

Terra mumbled, "Bite this, bitch," as she zipped up her parka.

Ozzy stifled a laugh and whispered, "Careful, she's not worth it."

Sayer scowled at Terra. "Thith ith how you handle the media? I believe an apology ith in order, Ms. Perez."

Ozzy gave Terra an encouraging, *make-nice* nod.

"I apologize, Ms. Teller," Terra said mechanically, through clinched teeth, "I don't know what I could have been—"

A low rumble sounded in the distance, then a thunderous boom, and a loud crack. The room shuddered from a series of sharp jolts. Swaying shelves dumped their contents on the floor.

Terra lost her balance.

Ozzy grabbed her. "What was that?" she said.

"Ice quake?" Lorelei said.

"Yeah, something like that. They're called cryoseisms, glacial ice moving over a rough patch in the bedrock. They happen fairly often. Never felt one *that* big before, though," Ozzy said.

Lorelei staggered over to Eaton's tarp covered cot like a seasick sailor and planted her heart-shaped butt down hard.

Oh shit.

Crunch.

She wiggled to get comfortable. Ozzy started to say something, but just smiled nervously instead.

Wish you were here, Ben. But I guess you are—in a fucked up way.

Darnell sauntered in.

Lorelei gave *him* the once over a couple of times.

"Hey, what's shakin'?" Darnell said.

No one laughed, but Terra gave him a consolation smile.

He turned to Sayer. "I bagged Dr. Eaton's body. He's good to go."

"What body?" Ozzy looked confused.

"Dr. Eaton. In the stairwell," Darnell said.

"He's not out there," Ozzy said.

"Then where in the hell ith he?" Sayer said.

Lorelei glanced up.

Ozzy pointed to where she sat. "Over there, on his cot, under the tarp."

Lorelei bolted to her feet, swatting imaginary corpse cooties off her heart-shaped ass.

"Don't worry, ma'am," Ozzy said, "Ben wouldn't mind." He searched for the right words, "He admired your work as a journalist more than you'll ever, ever know."

Sayer pulled the tarp off Eaton's remains.

Everyone gasped.

Maybe I should have said something earlier.

Clotted blood and icy suet caked Eaton's twisted mouth.

His mangled leg rested sideways across his sunken chest.

Lorelei smirked and opened the door. "Hey, my guys, grab your gear." She stepped through and slammed the door behind her.

Terra's eyes darted back and forth between Eaton's half-eaten leg and his gore-encrusted mouth. "That radio message back at EDI, Dr. Eaton wasn't saying I *hate* myself. He was saying I *ate* myself."

Sayer plopped down on the La-Z-Boy and put his head in his hands. "Perfect, that'th fucking perfect. E.D.I. thcientist eath himthelf in Antarctica. Film at eleven."

Terra led Ozzy to the door. "Let's get out of here before that witch comes back with her flying monkeys."

"Whoa, whoa, whoa, wait a minute" Sayer said, pointing to the door, "Who wath that out there?"

"One of the Red Wolf parka boys," Ozzy said.

"Who?"

"Two paramilitary nut jobs blew up our science station. Your guy in the crevasse was one of them." Ozzy pointed to the stairwell. "He must have been the other."

"Something ripped that dude to pieces, big time," Darnell said.

"Mutant penguins. They ripped the shit outta me." Ozzy pulled up his pant leg and showed his scars.

"I wonder if it was the thame one we—" Sayer said.

"*One?*" Ozzy said, "There are thousands of those vicious little freaks out there."

Darnell looked worried. "Bummer."

"Let's go," Terra said.

Sayer shooed them all out. "Go, go, go!"

Ozzy looked over his shoulder at Eaton's corpse.

"I promised I'd bury Ben in Florida," Ozzy said with a shrug.

Sayer called out to Darnell, "Get another body bag. Apparently, Dr. Eaton ith going to Florida."

Sayer glanced down at the floor by the TV, and picked up Poe and the Robonatrix. Ozzy grabbed them out of Sayer's hands and pulled them apart.

"Sorry Poe, you're comin' with me," Ozzy said.

Ozzy pocketed Poe and handed the Robonatrix back to Sayer. "She's all yours, Frank."

Sayer held the plastic beauty with her black leather straps and studs like she was a dead rat. "Isn't thith—"

"The Robonatrix," Terra said, "I had one when I was a kid."

"They thold that to children?" Sayer said.

Ozzy rummaged around under Eaton's cot and piled action figures on top of his friend's corpse.

Darnell returned with Roy, ears bandaged. Darnell carried a body bag over to Eaton's cadaver. He picked up an action figure next to Eaton's dismembered leg. "Whoooha, Leatherface. Does Dr. Eaton really need all these fine toys? I mean, like, after all he is—"

"No, no, you can have 'em," Ozzy said.

Roy picked up Elvis and flicked off a gory bit. "Can I—"

"He's all yours," Ozzy said.

"Thank you very much," Roy said, a la Elvis.

Sayer sighed, "A thouthand mileth from nowhere, thurrounded by total fucking idiotth."

Darnell and Roy zipped Eaton's body bag and carried it outside. Sayer herded everyone out.

Sayer scowled at Ozzy. "Aren't you forgetting thomething?"

"What?" Ozzy checked his pockets and looked around.

"The televithion—aren't you going to turn off the damn TV?"

Ozzy stiffened. "I—I'd really rather not, Frank. If you don't mind."

"Thuit yourthelf."

Ozzy paused at the door and took one last look at the Pit. He killed the lights and slammed the door. Ozzy smiled as the muffled voice of Alex Trebek quipped with contestants on *Jeopardy* in the cold, empty room.

It's up to you now, Alex, to keep the silence at bay at least until the generator runs out of gas.

Ozzy climbed the stairs a few steps behind Sayer—well aware of the horror lurking somewhere on the endless ice. Each step intensified the dread that overshadowed the excitement of his rescue.

Once on the ice he scanned the scene, and was surprised to see snow had cloaked any trace of carnage. The longest night on the planet was clear and calm, the stars so dense they almost equaled the pitch black surrounding them. The headlights of the three waiting Sno-Cats cast eerie shadows in the ruins of the science station. The group moved toward their vehicles. Even though none of them knew what Ozzy knew, they were cautious and jumpy.

The news crew filmed Roy and Darnell as they lifted Eaton's body bag into the back of Sayer's Sno-Cat.

Ride easy, buddy. Next stop Florida. I'm thinking some place inland like Gainesville. Wouldn't want sea level rise to interfere with the luxury of your natural decomposition.

"Okay, Michael Moore," Sayer said, as he held his hand over the camera lens, "Put a cap on it."

Chad sat behind the wheel of the supply Sno-Cat with the motor running. He eyeballed the ruins like a mouse in a house full of cats. A *screech* echoed in the distance. Chad ground the gears and took off by himself.

Ozzy ran after him. "Hey, wait up. We should stick together."

Oblivious Oblivion

A while later, Ozzy and Terra snuggled in the rear seat of Sayer's Sno-Cat like they were on a date, as the rescue party lumbered across the primordial ice.

Fifty yards ahead, the taillights of Chad's Sno-Cat turned the ice blood red.

Lorelei and her news crew followed close behind.

A constant stream of warm air circulated through the cabin of the hulking snow vehicle, but it couldn't compare to the warmth Ozzy felt inside with Terra's head on his shoulder. Ozzy thought he heard a *screech* cut through the throaty rumble of diesel engines, but Buster Pointdexter's *Feeling Hot Hot Hot* made it impossible to be sure.

Darnell drove Sayer's Sno-Cat, with the old man riding shotgun and Roy sitting between them.

Ozzy and Terra eavesdropped on the bickering trio on the front seat.

"No, hear me out—" Darnell said to Sayer.

"Forget about it. The penguinth are not alienth, they're thome kind of mutation or maybe they—"

"Everybody knows there are alien outposts in Antarctica."

Sayer said, "Ever heard about that, Roy?"

"That's news to me, mate."

"Okay, okay, but maybe the penguins were, like, exposed to an alien virus or something, from a meteor, or a comet, or space spores."

"Alien theorieth are like atholes, Darnell, everybody has one."

"It's just that, well, if those things were infected by some alien virus, then—then—oh forget it," said Darnel as he stared out the windshield.

"No, what?" said Sayer.

"Never mind. I'm just getting paranoid."

"About what?" Sayer said again.

Darnell blurted out, "*Roy.*"

"What'd I do?" Roy asked.

"Hey, you know I love you, man, but—"

"But what?" Roy said, more bored than annoyed.

"It's just that you were bitten by one of those things and maybe you...you..." Darnell searched for the right words.

"Oh, I get it, Roy ith one of *them* now." Sayer said.

"Whoa, like, you had suspicions too?"

I could tell them the mutants are radioactive, but where's the fun in that?

Roy jerked. His chest heaved. A bulge rose under his parka.

Darnell hugged the door.

The snaps on Roy's parka pop, pop, popped. Out came Roy's hand, his fingers forming a bird's head. "Cast aside your primitive human emotions. Together, we will build a gray new world free from the tyranny of love and desire," Roy's hand said, in a spooky little voice. Roy's bird-hand pecked Darnell's arm.

Darnell swatted at it.

They all laughed, except Darnell.

Okay, that was funny. Dumbass, but funny. I'm starting to like these guys.

The taillights of Chad's Sno-Cat disappeared.

Ozzy grabbed Darnell's shoulder. "Stop."

Darnell slammed on the breaks. "What the—"

The Sno-Cat groaned to a stop.

Darnell jumped out of the cab, ran thirty yards ahead and stopped.

Sayer, Roy, Ozzy and Terra ran toward him.

"What do you see?" Ozzy asked.

Darnell didn't answer. He just stood there, looking down. When the group reached him, they stopped in their tracks.

Can't see a damn thing.

Lorelei and her film crew joined the group. The cameraman pointed his camera down into the black below. The camera's LEDs illuminated a sheer vertical wall of ice plunging into pitch black. Waves crashed far, far below.

"I can't see anything," Terra said.

Ozzy put his hand on her shoulder and said, "Step back, Terra."

Terra held tight to Ozzy's arm. "Where's Chad?"

"He's gone."

"Down there?"

"Afraid so."

"Thit," said Sayer.

Darnell stared down into the darkness, "What *is* that down there?"

"The Ocean," Ozzy said.

"How can that be?" Terra said.

"Only one thing it could be—" said Roy.

"We're on an iceberg," Ozzy said.

"Oh—em—fucking—gee," Darnell said.

"The jolt we felt back in the Pit—it was part of the glacier calving off the ice sheet," said Ozzy, hoping his scientific curiosity would overcome his growing sense of dread.

Sayer waved to the group, "Let'th go."

"Like, where?" Darnell said.

"Anywhere but here," Sayer said, as he backed away from the edge.

"What about Chad?" Terra said in a quavering voice, "We can't just leave him down there."

Ozzy put his arm around Terra and said, "It's a 500 foot drop down to the ocean, maybe more. Chad could never survive a fall like that and if, somehow, he did, he'd only last a few minutes in the water. It's near freezing this time of year." Terra looked back over her shoulder as Ozzy led her back to the two remaining Sno-Cats.

Lorelei lingered at the edge of the frozen precipice. "Hey, my guys, let's do a set-up, right here."

Ozzy, Terra, Roy and Sayer climbed into the cab of their Sno-Cat.

Through the windshield, Ozzy watched Lorelei and her crew shoot a news segment. A song from Sayer's hot-theme set came on.

"Hand me the thatellite radio," Sayer said.

Ozzy searched the rear cargo area. Eaton's body was there. So were the automatic weapons. No satellite radio.

"Damn, the VSAT must have been in Chad's Sno-Cat," Ozzy said.

"Lorelei'th got a thatellite uplink," Sayer said.

Darnell cranked up the music and drummed on the steering wheel to quiet his nerves.

Ozzy said, "We can't hang around here any longer. It's too damn dangerous." He wiped condensation off the window and scanned the ice.

Abominations Abound

Out of the darkness, a legion of mutants waddled into the throw of the Sno-Cats' headlights. They converged on Lorelei and her crew.

Oh shit.

Ozzy kicked the back of Darnell's seat. "Heads up. They're here."

Darnell whipped around and scowled at Ozzy. "Who's here?"

Ozzy pointed outside. "That's who."

Darnell leaned on the horn.

The crew looked at him instead of the approaching mutants.

The creatures waddled as one undulating mass of snapping beaks and wriggling tentacles. The variety of their individual deformities defied classification. Some even had two heads, but they all had one thing in common—an uncontrollable drive to devour every living thing in their path. What they lacked in speed, they made up for in sheer numbers.

C'mon, c'mon, get the hell out of there. Run damnit.

Terra said, "Are those the bad penguins?"

She has no fucking idea.

"Oh yeah, but they're not penguins any more. They're black and white monstrosities."

"How many are there?"

"A few hundred too many."

"Do something—quick," Roy said.

Sayer bolted from the cab and called back to the others. "Follow me."

He yanked open the hatch to the rear cargo area of the

Sno-Cat and passed out Uzis to his crew.

Sayer turned to Ozzy, "Ever fire a gun like this before?"

"No," Ozzy said, "better gimme two."

Sayer handed Ozzy another Uzi, held his up and addressed the group, "Jutht pull back the bolt, thqueeze the trigger and don't point it at me."

"Never fired an Uzi, but I can handle an M-16," Roy said.

"I'm down with Uzis." Darnell said, "Hope we have beaucoup ammo. They're bullet hungry little fuckers."

Sayer offered an Uzi to Terra. "You don't have to take it."

"I don't like guns much, but if it has bullets and a trigger, I can shoot it. My father was a gun nut." She released the butt-stock and rested it on her hip. "Ready when you are."

You are fucking ready, aren't you?

Sayer passed out extra 32 round magazines.

The mutant horde surrounded Lorelei and her crew, backing them toward the cliff.

Ozzy bounded from the cab and hit the ground firing. Spent brass rained down in erratic arcs and sizzled on the glassy ice. He crossed his wrists, blowing away freaks in two directions at once. He pivoted left—right—firing to *Blister in the Sun*. The Uzis' report amped up the urgency of the Violent Femmes' syncopated beat. The creatures exploded in clouds of feathers and bloody bits.

Sayer, Darnell, Roy and Terra watched Ozzy in amazement.

He did a backward duck-walk and took out the last four mutants.

Ozzy grinned and blew on his two smoking barrels. "Sweet."

Sayer gave Ozzy a sideways glance. "You thaid you never fired one before."

"Yeah, I always use *two*." Ozzy grinned. "I was the Caltech paintball champion two years running."

Lorelei and her crew huddled on the edge of the iceberg. No one wanted to be the first to scream, but the terror in their eyes was deafening.

Sayer jogged toward them. "C'mon, c'mon. Get the hell out of there."

A *screech* echoed in the distance. Then another. Then surround-sound screeching.

Sayer swept his flashlight toward the sound.

Mutants converged from all directions.

"Haul ath!" Sayer said.

They all made a mad dash for the Sno-Cats. The mutants cut them off.

Ozzy opened fire and mowed down a swath of mutants, clearing a bloody path between Sayer's group and their vehicles. Their boots barely touched the ice as they tromped over the dead and dying monstrosities.

One of the near-dead creatures wrapped its wriggling tentacles around Sayer's ankle and sent him tumbling to the ice. The bullet-riddled abomination had enough life left to rip though Sayer's snow pants and gulp down a beak-full of insulation before falling dead on the red ice.

Sayer kicked at the deformed corpse with unnecessary fervor as more mutants advanced.

Terra bolted from Ozzy's side and rushed to help Sayer.

Ozzy sprayed bullets as he took off after her.

Terra pulled Sayer to his feet and toggled her Uzi to semi-automatic. She picked off mutants one by one, like cast-iron ducks in a carnival shooting gallery, but the creatures just kept coming.

As Ozzy fought his way to Terra and Sayer, a mutant jumped for her face.

Ozzy blasted it in mid-air with a hip-shot.

Darnell emptied his magazine. "I'm like all out, bro."

Ozzy pulled a fresh mag from his parka and tossed it to Darnell.

He slammed it into his weapon and said, "Much grass."

Darnell and Roy headed toward Ozzy, Terra and Sayer.

Ozzy waved them away. "You can make it to the Sno-Cat. Go, go, go. I can't see shit. Turn on the searchlight and blast the fuckers from the roof of the cab."

Roy and Darnell inched their way toward the Sno-Cat, firing back to back.

Three mutants plunged their beaks in Roy's leg. He stomped them into giblets.

"Dude, Riverdance the motherfuckers," Darnell said, striking a Michael Flatly pose.

Lorelei's cameraman filmed Sayer as he fired on the run.

A two-headed mutant leaped for Sayer's face.

He throttled one of their throats. The other head snapped at his hand.

Sayer head-butted the freakish creature and flung it with a force borne of anger and disgust. The mutant continued snapping as it sailed over Ozzy's head.

Through a blizzard of feathers, Darnell and Roy laid down cover fire as they scrambled up to the roof of the cab.

Roy switched on a roof-mounted searchlight.

The powerful beam illuminated Lorelei and her crew at the edge of the iceberg.

Shit. They're completely cut off.

Lorelei bludgeoned mutants with a microphone boom.

Her cameraman writhed in agony on the ice. Most of his mouth was gone, but that didn't prevent him from screaming.

Mutant penguins ripped an eye from its socket and fought each other for the shiny prize. The abandoned video camera recorded the vicious mutants ripping its terrified operator to shreds.

Ozzy hoisted Terra on his shoulders. She blasted mutants from a better angle as Ozzy shot and kicked his way toward the Sno-Cat.

Sayer seemed oddly composed as he methodically sprayed the hellish freaks with lead disinfectant.

There was nothing Ozzy could do to stop mutants from disemboweling the rest of Lorelei's crew. Ozzy looked away as the little monsters gorged themselves on the crew's internal organs. He scanned the area. Darnell and Roy fired and shouted from the roof of the Sno-Cat.

"Alien bastards," Darnell said, "No offense."

"Shut up," Roy said.

Sayer backed up toward the cab door, firing madly. "I'm running out of ammo."

"Haul ass for the cab, Frank," Roy said, "We got this."

Darnell and Roy blasted creatures as Sayer bolted for the cab, and dove inside.

Ozzy fought his way toward the Sno-Cat.

Mutants jammed the door.

Sayer slammed the door shut.

Crunch.

He gave a thumbs up to Ozzy as he slid behind the wheel.

Ozzy looked around for Lorelei and saw her fight off a cadre of mutants with her mike boom. She swung wide.

Several of the creatures and her mike boom soared up and over the edge of the ice cliff.

Lorelei lost her balance, fell, and slid toward the edge of oblivion like a curling stone. She dug her fingernails into the ice and stopped—her legs dangling over the edge. As she clawed her way back, a little freak pulled off her wig.

More mutants arrived and tore her wig to pieces. A penguin ripped through her parka, snipped a small hole in Lorelei's belly and emerged with a loop of her intestines. It yanked out a couple of feet. Lorelei grabbed her end.

"We have to go back, Ozzy," Terra said, "I hate her guts, but I don't want to see them all over the place."

It's too dangerous. I can't let anything happen to you.

Ozzy pushed ahead toward the Sno-Cat. "She's history, Terra. We're almost there."

Terra said. "Hold still a minute, darling."

She held her breath and took a single shot at the mutant playing tug-of-war with Lorelei's intestines.

Blood and black feathers spattered Lorelei's face. She stumbled to her feet cradling her viscera like a slippery new-born baby.

Terra hopped down from Ozzy's shoulders and took off toward Lorelei.

Ozzy said, "Come back here, damnit," and chased after her.

He caught up with her, and together they blasted their way to Lorelei.

When they reached Lorelei, she held up her intestines and said, "My guts came out."

Ozzy reached out to Lorelei. "Hop on my back."

Lorelei extended a bloody hand.

Ozzy hoisted her up.

Sayer's Sno-Cat rumbled toward the stranded trio, grinding mutants into the ice.

Another wave of mutants advanced.

Darnell and Roy blasted them back, from atop the cab.

Sayer's Sno-Cat lurched and stopped inches from Ozzy's feet.

Sayer opened the door for Ozzy, "Need a ride?"

"No thanks, Frank. I need the exercise."

I'll hold them back for as long as I can, until everyone is safely inside.

Roy climbed down from the roof to the hood of the Sno-Cat.

Ozzy handed his guns to Lorelei. He reached back and pushed Lorelei's ass up and over his head.

Terra maneuvered her onto the hood and kept her from sliding off.

Roy grabbed the back of Lorelei's parka and held her steady on the hood.

Darnell lay down fire until he emptied his magazine. "Dude, I'm out again."

Roy patted his pockets—empty. He tossed his gun to Darnell.

It sailed into Darnell's hands. "Nice throw, dude."

"Nice catch, ass clown."

The creatures advanced on Ozzy and Terra. She opened fire.

Ozzy said, "Go with Roy."

"You first," She said with a determined scowl.

That's not happening.

Ozzy hoisted Terra on the hood as Darnell pulled Lorelei to the roof of the cab, with him.

Terra tried to climb back down to Ozzy, but Roy wrapped his massive arms around her and said, "At the moment, you're the only one with a bloody gun, so I suggest you shoot it."

Terra stood up and picked off the mutant's nearest Ozzy.

Roy called up to Darnell, "Where are the guns the news lady had, mate? I need one now."

Darnell yanked both Uzis from Lorelei's hands. The guns were hopelessly tangled in her intestines. He squeezed off a few rounds as he struggled to untangle the slippery mess. Lorelei tried to help. They both fumbled with her bowels.

Mutants converged on Ozzy and the Sno-Cat. One leaped on the hood—then another—and another.

Roy kicked them off.

More hopped on.

Roy tugged Terra's arm. "C'mon, let's go up top."

Ozzy said, "Do what he says. I'll be right behind you."

"You better," Terra said and tossed Ozzy her Uzi.

Roy tried to help up.

"Does it look like my arms are broken?" she said as she scrambled to the roof of the cab.

Once on top, she extended her hand to help Roy up. He grinned and took it.

The devil birds on the hood pecked the windshield.

Ozzy looked on with frustration, as Terra's legs dangled outside the passenger side window.

"For fuck's sake, Frank, do something."

Inside the cab, Sayer rolled down the passenger side window and guided Terra inside, then Lorelei, then Roy and Darnell.

Out on the ice, the creatures swarmed Ozzy. He fired until his ammo ran out. A wild-eyed mutant charged with a gaping maw, and Ozzy shoved the Uzi's molten barrel down its throat.

The smoldering attacker screeched and wrapped its tentacles around the gun's nut cap. That was hot too and the wriggling appendages curled up like earthworms on a sweltering sidewalk.

The smell of seared flesh incited the mutants to attack with even greater ferocity.

Ozzy choked his Uzi's butt stock and swung like drunken slugger in a weekend pick-up game. He pummeled mutants without mercy, but more kept on coming. He stomped and kicked the ones that eluded his deadly swing, but it was a losing battle.

If I can just hold these fuckers off for a little while longer, the others can get the hell out of here.

Ozzy waved to Sayer. "Forget about me. Haul ass."

I suppose there are worse ways to die, but I can't think of any right now.

The penguins ripped open Ozzy's parka. His Poe action figure tumbled to the ice.

A mutant took off with it.

Ozzy grabbed the beast by the flippers. He raised it until they were eyeball to eyeball.

"Drop it," Ozzy said.

The mutant dropped the action figure and snapped at Ozzy's nose.

He windmilled the creature and let go.

The little monster flapped its stubby wings as it tumbled through the air. It hit the ice hard and scurried away.

Ozzy snatched Poe from the ice and stuffed him in his pocket.

They almost got you, Edgar. You scared yet?

Frantic screeches and shrieks sounded beyond the throw of the searchlight beam. The mutants nearest Ozzy turned around. He strained to see what was going on, but darkness obscured the outermost swarm of the gathering horde. The shrill cacophony grew nearer.

Something plowed through the mutant colony, flinging mangled creatures up and over the heads of nearby attackers. It was if there was an unseen path of carnage that was heading straight for him.

What the fuck is going on here?

A long, wailing cry cut through the frantic screeching of the horde—then the kind of guttural growl that dead things hear in the instant of their death. It sounded good to Ozzy—better than good—it sounded like a wolf.

In a heartbeat, Rufus ripped into the monstrosities surrounding Ozzy. He gasped at the wolf's ferocity as the beast ripped the mutants apart with the kind of fury he felt when he went berserk on the commandos. One by one, the snarling wolf's merciless jaws gnawed the advancing abominations into screeching meat.

You're no spirit animal, Rufus. You're a fucking killing machine.

Glimpses of bloody fangs and flying gore flashed in the searchlight's beam. Rufus' eyes burned wild with terrifying purpose. His keen ears swept back against his broad cranium. Inside that thick, bone dome, Ozzy sensed a single thought occupied the perfect predator's brain. Kill the freaks. Kill them all.

Ozzy envied Rufus' berserker, blood lust, but sadly, it wasn't going to be enough. The mutants just kept coming. They waddled up and over the mound of dismembered corpses. Mutant blood spattered from Rufus' snarling mouth. A mound of mutilated mutants encircled man and wolf.

Rufus hunched down in total exhaustion. He panted and rested his blood-soaked snout on Ozzy's gore encrusted boot.

Ozzy knelt beside Rufus and put his arm around the beast's powerful neck.

Another wave of mutants approached from all directions.

"We're done here, Rufus. Too many of those little fuckers. We're done, but you won't be dying on a stainless-steel table—not this time. We'll do this together."

Not too far away he could hear Terra calling out to him. "I love you, Ozzy. Don't leave me. Please don't leave me."

Ozzy hoisted Rufus on his shoulders and rose to his feet with great effort. He stood defiant and faced the screeching fiends surrounding them. As Ozzy struggled under the weight of the wolf, the albino skull talisman protruded from a rip in his parka. It emerged from its down covered hole and hung low on Ozzy's chest. The mutants stopped advancing when they saw it.

Ozzy grinned. "You're not going to like this, Rufus—trust me."

He raised the skull to his lips and blew into its neck-hole.

Shriek.

Rufus yelped.

The screeching horde fell silent.

Ozzy blew the talisman again—*shriek*.

The mutants retreated in an ever-widening circle. A clear path opened up between Ozzy and the Sno-Cat.

Sayer maneuvered his Sno-Cat toward Ozzy.

The horde advanced.

Ozzy took a deep breath and blew on the skull again—only a faint *squeak* came out.

The Sno-Cat ground to a stop near Ozzy.

Darnell threw open the cab door, and said, "Dude, where did you get the badass dog?"

Darnell helped Ozzy slide Rufus onto the backseat. Terra recoiled as the wolf leaped into the cargo area, and curled up on top of Eaton's body bag.

"That's no dog, mate. I know a bleeding wolf when I see one," Roy said to Darnell.

Ozzy climbed in the backseat and scooted next to Terra. She squeezed his hand so hard, his knuckles popped. "You had me scared there for a while."

Ozzy wrenched his hand out of Terra's death grip and put his arm around her. "So, what you said when you thought I was going to die—"

Terra brushed some bloody feathers from his hair. "I wouldn't have said it if I didn't mean it."

"Well, the feeling's more than mutual, but I have to warn you. That wolf back there, I fucking love him too. Rufus is my ah-ah spirit animal."

"I'm no expert on all that spirity stuff, but he looks more like an animal-animal, to me," Darnell said.

Sayer slammed the Sno-Cat into gear, and drove off in the opposite direction of the cliff and the mutants. The tracks of the Sno-Cat pulverized the screeching monstrosities into crimson slush.

Terra helped Ozzy out of his bloody parka. A roadmap of cuts and scratches covered his muscular chest.

"Ouch," Terra said, "You okay?"

"Yeah, but I'm gonna be sore as hell tomorrow."

Ozzy handed his Edgar Allan Poe action figure to Terra. "I want you to have this, Terra."

Terra accepted the bloody toy like it was a dozen roses. "Thank you, Ozzy."

Lorelei smoothed out the kinks in her intestines, with great care and determination.

"What do we do now?" Roy said.

Sayer reached back as he steered and shook Lorelei's knee. "Where'th your uplink?"

Lorelei stuck a fistful of viscera in his face. "My guts came out."

"Give me the coordinateth to the abandoned chopper," Sayer said to Roy.

Homeward Hearts

When they arrived at the landing site, a light still glowed inside the chopper's cabin. Ozzy grabbed two Uzis, fed fresh mags to the hungry hand grips, and bounded onto the ice—an Uzi in each hand. His chest was bare except for the mutant skull tied around his neck.

Rufus leaped over the back seat and limped to Ozzy's side.

Terra and Sayer helped Lorelei out of the Sno-Cat as Darnell and Roy unloaded Eaton's corpse from the back and lugged it to the chopper.

Ozzy and Rufus scanned the ice as the others climbed into the helicopter.

Rufus will smell those monster's stink long before I see them.

"Okay, Rufus, looks like those fuckers have moved on, so let's get out of here."

Once everyone was safely inside, Ozzy lifted Rufus to his chest and staggered toward the open door. Rufus growled and leaped from his arms.

"Oh, I get it, you think colonel fuck head is inside. That maniac is mutant shit by now, buddy."

Terra leaned out the door and called to Rufus, "C'mon, Mr. wolf. Who's a g'boy?"

Rufus looked at Ozzy, then at Terra who was smiling and clapping. He approached the open door, with keen, canine trepidation.

Ozzy lifted Rufus up high enough for the suspicious beast to inspect the chopper's spacious interior.

Terra put her arms around the wolf's neck.

Sayer said, "Are you thure thath thafe?"

"He knows she's with me, Frank. He's a Buddha wolf. They know that kinda shit," Ozzy said as he hoisted Rufus inside.

Ozzy climbed aboard, shivering, and slid the door shut.

Roy and Darnell hoisted Eaton's body bag into the webbing that ran the length of the rear bulkhead of the chopper. They ambled back into the cabin, and plopped down on two, white leather swivel chairs opposite the long sofa where Terra and Lorelei sat.

Sayer settled into the pilot's seat and fiddled with the instruments in the cockpit.

Roy swiveled his chair, leaned in the cockpit doorway, and said, "Can you actually fly this bloody thing?"

"Hey, I flew a Huey in the Gulf," Sayer said, "It'th like riding a bike."

Roy scratched his head, "Did the bicycles in Baghdad have all those switches and gauges and shit?"

Ozzy scooted next to Terra on the couch.

She reached for his guns and said, "Let me take those for you, darling."

Ozzy beamed and shrugged off the gun straps. He took a deep breath, and looked around for Rufus. The wolf nibbled bits and pieces of the commandos that littered the cabin floor. The contrast between the stark white decor and the bright red gore made the interior look like a strawberry sundae from hell.

Terra said, "I thought wolves didn't eat people."

"They don't. Does that bloody chum look like person to you?" Ozzy said.

"Guess not," she kicked a fleshy bit in the wolf's direction, "But that kinda looked like a nose."

Rufus gobbled up the morsel and gazed at Terra for a long moment.

"See, he likes you."

"I like him, too, but he is, ya know, a wolf."

"Well yeah, but dogs are pretty wolfish if you think about it."

"Is he your wolf, mate?" Roy said.

"No, It's more like I'm his human."

Terra walked over to Rufus and scratched his head as he chomped away at the frozen meat and said, "Okay then, I'll be your human, too."

Ozzy peeked in the open cockpit door. "How goes it, Frank?"

"I jutht about have it figured out."

"Better hurry," Darnell said, "Isn't this iceberg, like, melting?"

Ozzy laughed. "These things are ginormous. It could take years to melt."

"Hey, let's call it something," Terra said.

"Too bad Iceland's already taken," Roy said.

Ozzy felt a tap on his shoulder. He glanced over at Lorelei cradling her intestines. She had scooted next to him on the sofa. She held up her slippery mess, and said, "My guts came out."

Ozzy nodded and leaned away. "You can say that again."

Terra said, "Oh, she will—that's *all* she says."

Ozzy said, "Hey, Darnell—a little help here. This woman requires some fucking medical attention."

Darnell went into medic mode and made Lorelei lie down on the sofa.

Terra and Ozzy scrunched together to make room.

Darnell checked the contents of his medical kit. "I got everything I need—except morphine."

Lorelei held up her intestines. "My—"

"I know, baby, your guts came out. I'm gonna do something about that right now, but I'm afraid we're gonna have to do this straight."

Darnell unzipped her parka and cut open her blouse.

Her intestines protruded from a small hole in the left side of her remarkably buff abdomen.

"What is *this*? Does the bodacious news babe have a girly six-pack?" Darnell said.

Lorelei gazed up at him and flashed her trademark smirky smile.

"I think she does." Darnell winked and swabbed antiseptic on Lorelei's stomach with a cotton ball.

Roy wandered over to take a peek. "Killer abs."

"Dude, do you mind? This is a doctor-patient moment," Darnell said.

"Doctor my ass." Roy turned to Lorelei and lifted the bloody bandages from around his ears. "Would a real doctor do this?" Darnell had sewn Roy's ears on backwards.

"As if, man. It was dark, okay." Darnell whispered to Lorelei, "He's, like, not of this world, you know."

Darnell squirted antiseptic on Lorelei's intestines and stuffed them back in the tiny hole. "This really isn't that bad. No tears or punctures. No evidence of ischemia."

Lorelei fussed with Darnell's spikey hair as he stuffed her intestines back where they belonged. One small loop remained. Darnell poked it back in with his index finger. Lorelei responded with a sensuous sigh.

Darnell rummaged around in his medical kit. "A few sutures, some Ampicillin and you'll be as good as—"

Lorelei pulled Darnell toward her. The medical kit crashed to the floor. They all gawked as Lorelei grabbed the back of Darnell's neck and tongue fucked the unsuspecting medic. He recoiled, at first, then returned the favor.

Ozzy did a double take.

Eaton's grim cadaver loomed over the unlikely lovebirds and glared back at Ozzy.

Seriously, are you going to haunt me for the rest of my life?

Terra made a prune face, "Oh—my—god."

"You see him too?" Ozzy said.

"Yeah, gross." She shuddered. "How can Darnell kiss that spooky hoochie?"

Ozzy looked back at Eaton—he was gone.

Screech.

Ozzy peered out a side window. The Sno-Cat's searchlight revealed a swarm of mutants advancing on their helicopter.

Sayer called out from the cockpit, "Hey, Ozzy—"

Ozzy poked his head in the cockpit.

Sayer pointed to a red switch. "What doeth the tiny type

thay? I can't find my reading glatheth. I think I left them back at the—"

"Whoa, maybe we should just get on the radio and—"

"C'mon, c'mon, what the fuck doeth it thay?"

"Magnetos," answered Ozzy.

Sayer grinned, and threw the switch. The Cougar 100's twin jet engines roared to life. Ozzy strapped himself into the co-pilot's seat as the chopper's massive rotor gyrated ever faster.

Out on the ice, hundreds of mutants surrounded the helicopter. The hungry little horrors blew away in all directions, as the whirling leviathan hurtled upward, and streaked away, like a shooting star, into the vast polar sky.

Epilogue

West Flanders, Belgium—Five Years Later

Nathan felt out of place in the leathered and burled interior of a Mercedes-Benz limousine. As the long, white limo sped past postcard perfect pastures, complete with windmills, he rifled the pocket his off-the-rack suit, and pulled out an engraved nametag.

This thing is solid platinum. Nathan J. Harper, PhD— Science Minister. What a joke. Associate junior college professor would be more like it. For the kind of money they're paying me, they can call me whatever they want.

Nathan opened the console refrigerator and frowned when he looked inside.

Damn, nothing but Dom Perignon.

He pulled out a couple of the chilly, green bottles and smiled.

That's more like it.

He grabbed a can of Coke, flipped the top, poured some into a crystal champagne flute, and held it high.

Here's to megalomaniacs with money—where ever you are.

Nathan unplugged the charger and opened his laptop. A PowerPoint presentation entitled "Cryonova" filled the screen.

Powered up and ready to rock.

He took a sip of Coke and slid the laptop into his bag.

Nathan's limo pulled into a circular, cobblestone driveway

that snaked its way to the kind of chateau that probably had stables in the back and a ghost in a dormer window. He was not the first to arrive. In fact, there were so many other limos and exotic sports cars clogging the driveway that he had to hoof it fifty yards to the grand entryway. From the uppermost parapet of the imposing structure, the red wolf flag of L'ordre Du Loup Rouge fluttered in the tepid breeze.

Once inside, a cadre of armed commandos escorted Nathan to a cavernous dining hall. A cabal of slick Euroguys, wearing expensive suits, sat around an ultra-modern conference table. They smoked, and whispered, and nursed the drinks an army of domestics served with overly formal flair. Nathan was last to take a seat. The others paid him no attention and he was certain he had never met any of them before. Each man had a name plaque in front of him—minister this and minister that. He couldn't help but notice there wasn't a single woman in attendance.

Whose sausage party is this anyway?

A jittery-eyed man glided through a service door at rear of the hall like a timid ghost. He fiddled with the ministers' laptops, bowing before moving on to the next one. He approached Nathan without making eye-contact, tapped in a code on his laptop keyboard, and linked it to an enormous monitor that hovered above a bronze bust.

Shit, that's King Leopold II up there. That monster killed millions of Africans in the Congo at the end of the nineteenth century.

The monitor flickered and the word CRYONOVA, in an overly arty font, flashed on the giant screen. No one noticed. All eyes were on the colossal, mahogany double doors at the opposite end of the hall.

The doors burst open. Light flooded the darkened room. Colonel Pomeroy entered, flanked by two commandos wearing dress white uniforms. The Colonel scuttled in on a robotic life-support module. A casual observer could easily mistake the contraption for portable steam bath with a variety of baffling accessories. Nathan had a pretty good idea that some of the add-ons were weapons. Even from across the room the glossy, white machine smelled like an ICU.

A Dalek would envy that rig.

One of the commandos stepped forward, clicked his heels, and said, "Hail Pomeroy, Grand Commandant of L'ordre Du Loup Rouge."

The assembled ministers stood at attention and saluted Roman style, which was way too Naziesque for Nathan, so he pretended to do something important on his laptop.

The only vestiges of the colonel's humanity were the remnants of his mutant ravaged face—much of which was shadowed by a white pith helmet. The commandos slammed the doors shut and positioned themselves on either side.

The intelligence minister was the first to speak. "Welcome back, mon colonel."

This guy looks like a Bond villain.

Humming motors and gurgling fluids echoed in the cavernous room as Colonel Pomeroy's cyborg contraption maneuvered to the head of the table. "Be seated, s'il vous plait."

The security minister said, "You are looking quite...fit, Colonel."

Why does he seem so nervous?

"Enough, Maurice. You know what I want."

The security minister nodded and offered him a plate. "Sardines?"

"No, no, no, Imbecile—Dr. Pratt. Where is he now?"

Okay, that's why he's so nervous.

"Much has changed since you were taken from us, Colonel," the intelligence minister said, "You might say Dr. Pratt and his associates have been at sea these past five years."

The intelligence minister controlled a PowerPoint presentation from his laptop computer. A satellite photo of an enormous iceberg surrounded by open ocean filled the projection screen.

Wonder where they got that picture. They can't have their own satellite.

"I do not understand," the colonel said, "I see no boat."

"Dr. Pratt is not on a boat. He is on that iceberg. B38, to be exact. It is currently at 32 degrees north latitude, 132 degrees west longitude."

"And where, pray tell, is that?"

The projection changed to a satellite image of the iceberg off the west coast of the United States.

"872 miles west of San Diego, California."

"This is absurd. Surely an iceberg would have melted by now."

Okay, I got this.

"When B38 calved off the Antarctic ice sheet, it was roughly 140,000 square kilometers, a bit larger than Greece," Nathan said, with professorial authority, "If they keep heading north, to colder waters, it may never melt."

"The American government, have they not taken control of such a thing?" asked the colonel.

"No, no they cannot," the security minister said, "It is in international waters."

The foreign minister added, "Over 60 countries recognize them as a sovereign nation."

"Absurd. How is this possible?"

"The Earthwatch One survivors claimed salvage rights on all the abandoned science stations on B38.

The intelligence minister added, "Then they declared B38 a sovereign nation and named it Cryonova."

"Pour quoi?"

"So they could do their...their weird science," the security minister said.

"They have created a safe haven for clandestine scientific research." The intelligence minister said.

The finance minister added, "It is also extremely profitable. Last year, Cryonova had a G.N.P. of eight billion Euros, colonel. And they use it to fund any environmental group with a logo and a letterhead."

The intelligence minister changed the projection to an aerial view of buildings. "They derive most of their revenue from these biotech facilities." He aimed a laser pointer. "Here,

here and here are the laboratories where they conduct their stem cell and cloning research and that's where they manufacture their pharmaceuticals."

That's not the half of it.

"The Americans lost many of their top geneticists to Cryonova," Nathan said, "including four Nobel laureates."

The intelligence minister aimed his laser pointer. "Here's the clinic where they perform their stem cell based therapies."

Nathan turned to Colonel Pomeroy. "Perhaps *you* would benefit from Dr. Pratt's medical breakthroughs."

"I have Dr. Pratt and his penguins to thank for my present condition. Now, it is his turn to learn the indignities of the flesh."

If you say so. No one briefed me on any penguins.

"The doctor has friends in high places," the intelligence minister said, "Take a look at these surveillance photos of patients entering his clinic."

Grainy photos flash on the projection screen. "The Russian president, the German chancellor —"

"There, in the sunglasses, is that not—"

"Reverend Loudermilk. The American evangelist who preaches the evils of science."

Nice hair.

"I'm not sure if I should show this last photo." the intelligence minister said.

"Now you *must* show it," the colonel demanded.

The intelligence minister tapped his laptop keyboard. The projection changed to a photo of Maurice, the security minister, hugging Ozzy Pratt. All eyes glared at Maurice.

Nathan laughed.

Colonel Pomeroy scowled at the security minister. "So, now you fraternize with my enemies, Maurice?"

"Do you know what it is like to lose someone you love more than life its self?" Maurice said.

The colonel almost looked concerned. "Not your wife, I hope. Did she—"

"No, no, no, she is well." Maurice said, "It's my Binki. He...

he chewed through a power cord and...and..."

"Tell me the head of security for L'ordre Du Loup Rouge did not clone his fru-fru poodle dog."

Don't laugh. Whatever you do, don't fucking laugh. These guys are crazy.

"I cannot do that, mon Colonel," Maurice said, as sweat stains widened under the arms of his Valentino suit.

Maurice's hands shook as he pulled a snapshot of a slobbering poodle puppy from his wallet and held it up. "My sweet, sweet little Binki Boy. They brought him back to me."

"Collaborator," the colonel said.

A single shot rang out.

A clean round hole in the center of the photo, framed Maurice, with a much larger and far less tidy hole in the middle of his forehead. His body crumpled in a heap on the parquet floor.

Nathan scanned the room.

The other ministers brushed bits of Maurice's brain from their expensive suits, so Nathan figured it was okay to wiped a glob of gray matter from his cheek.

I have to get the fuck out of here.

A wisp of smoke rose from a gun barrel projecting from Colonel Pomeroy's contraption, "Are there any more photographs you should not show to me?"

The ministers looked at each other and they all shook their heads in unison.

"*Très bien,*" the colonel said, "Now let us discuss our plans for the resourceful Dr. Pratt."

The Sovereign Nation of Cryonova—Somewhere in the Pacific

Ozzy, with Rufus by his side, looked out a towering wall of windows at the lush hanging gardens and walkways that rose above the ice. The spacious living room was a modern masterpiece of glass and steel construction.

Down below, Darnell sunned himself beside a San Simeon-sized pool.

On the distant ice, Roy commanded a vast legion of mutant penguins. Each creature wore a sonic headset that compelled them to mirror Roy's every move.

Ozzy turned his attention to a gigantic television screen when Lorelei came on the news. Frank Sayer pushed a man in a wheelchair through the front door of a clinic. They smiled and waved to the camera as Lorelei reported, "President Sayer met with British Prime Minister Lloyd today after his successful treatment for pancreatic cancer."

In the living room, a scrawny toddler wearing droopy diapers, ambled over to the colossal screen. He put his little hands on Lorelei's huge lips as she spoke. "The Prime Minister assured President Sayer that Great Britain would be the first G-Eight country to recognize Cryonova as a sovereign nation."

Terra sashayed into the living room wearing a sundress and a floppy hat. She scooped the toddler up. "C'mon sweetie, let's go bye-bye."

The toddler squirmed out of her arms and said, "Stop talking to me like that. I am not now, nor will I ever be your *sweetie*."

Ozzy said. "Hey, I heard that." He ruffled the toddler's wild red hair. "Chill the fuck out, Ben. Show Terra some respect. Technically, she *is* your mother. After all, she carried your scrawny ass for nine—"

"My apologizes—*Mommy*," the toddler said. "It won't happen again. Okay?"

Terra smiled. "Oh, that's okay, sweetie."

Ozzy said, "Let's all check out the baby mammoth. He's already—"

"What you can do is take me to see Lorelei, Ozzy." The toddler stomped his foot and pointed to the screen.

"As you can see, she's kinda busy right now, Ben," Ozzy said, "We'll hook up with her later, but only if you promise to follow the rules."

"Okay, okay," the toddler said. "I'll try to act my damn age. Goo goo ga ga. Satisfied?"

"That's much better. You know the consequences if this

blows the fuck up before we have a chance to get to the bottom of your biological memory transmission. It's going to be a—"

"I keep telling Dr. Lee that it's some kind of unknown epigenetic mechanism in the cloned DNA, but she won't let me work on it with her," Ben said.

"I'll talk with her, but I have to tell ya, you freak her the fuck out."

"I never asked to be cloned."

"Hello—you were dead."

"About that. I'm not ready to talk about it, but when I do, you'll be the one with crap in his pants."

"I'll crap my pants if Dr. Lee rushes to publish," Ozzy said, "For all we know, she's been in contact with China, all along."

"I seriously doubt it. Not when there's a Nobel Prize with her name on it, but only if we handle this properly."

"Yeah, if we don't, the UN will shut us down, pronto," Ozzy said.

Terra walked over and tugged Ozzy's tee-shirt. "C'mon, boys, let's not waste this beautiful day."

Terra and Ozzy each held one of the toddler's tiny hands as all three headed for the door, with Rufus close behind. As they left, little Ben gazed back over his shoulder at Lorelei on the big screen.

"This is Lorelei Teller for Dateline Cryonova." The corner of her mouth rose—ever so slightly.

About the Author

Robert Payne Cabeen is a screenwriter, artist, purveyor of narrative horror poetry, and now a novelist. His screenwriting credits include *Heavy Metal 2000*, for Columbia/TriStar, Sony Pictures, *A Monkey's Tale*, and *Walking with Buddha*.

Cabeen's illustrated book *Fearworms: Selected Poems* was a 2015 Bram Stoker Award nominee.

As creative director for Streamline Pictures, Robert helped anime pioneer Carl Macek bring Japanese animated features, like *Akira* and dozens of other classics, to a western audience.

Cabeen received a Master of Fine Arts degree from Otis Art Institute, with a dual major in painting and design. Since then, he has combined his interests in the visual arts with screenwriting and storytelling for a broad range of entertainment companies including Warner Brothers, Columbia/TriStar, Disney, Sony, Universal, USA Network, Nelvana and SEGA.

Robert is a city of Lost Angels native. He resides in the Miracle Mile with his wife Cecile Grimm. Together, they spawned three offspring—all smarter, better looking and more talented than he is—but certainly not as scary.

For more about Robert Payne Cabeen, visit: robertpaynecabeen.com

MUTANT SKETCHBOOK

concept art by
Robert Payne Cabeen

The creature leaped at Ozzy's face, feet first, with its enormous talons splayed for attack.

The penguin tossed his head back and Roy's ear disappeared into its gullet.

The brutish bird looked like no animal Ozzy had ever seen, with its cranial fin, deep-set eyes, huge talons, and sharp bone spurs on the end of its flippers. It had a burly, upper-body musculature that was totally un-avian. As monstrous as the brute looked, it smelled even worse.

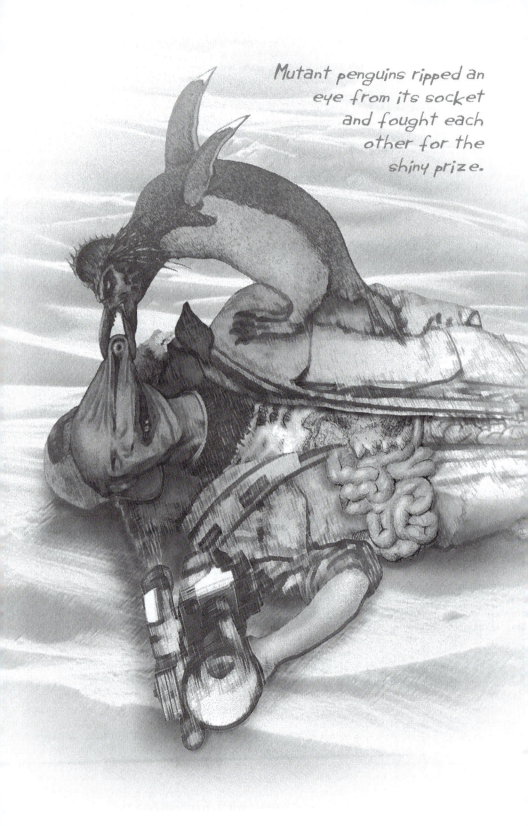

Mutant penguins ripped an eye from its socket and fought each other for the shiny prize.

A penguin, with tentacles
protruding from tumorous lesions
below its snapping beak, attacked Ozzy from
behind. Its serpentine appendages wrapped around
his knee and slithered up his inner thigh. Ozzy
whipped around as the creature pinned his thigh
with its sharp, flipper spurs, snapping and snipping,
as its tentacles constricted tighter and tighter.

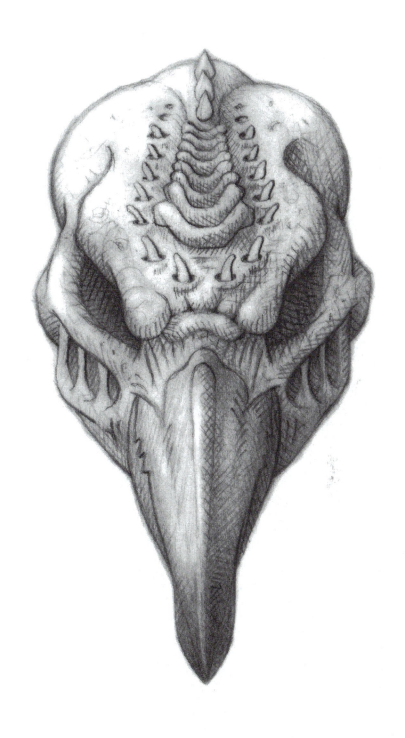

"Do you suppose radiation is causing normal penguins to mutate?"

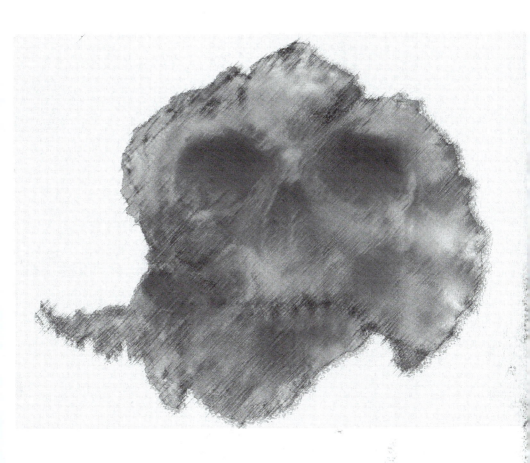

"For some, Antarctica is the last frontier, a land of frigid beauty and adventure. But when the murderous Antarctic wind rips down the immense south polar ice dome, and slashes across the vast frozen desert like a thousand maniacs, adventure can end in a cold and lonely grave."

—Lorelei Teller